To:
Dale Schwartz

Mustafa
9/30/10

The Surrogate

The Surrogate

Mustafa Abubaker

To order additional copies of this book, contact:
Xlibris Corporation
1-888-795-4274
www.Xlibris.com
Orders@Xlibris.com
66494

CONTENTS

To Grandpa who taught me how to be a man

ISLAMABAD, 1990

I looked at you and saw Raiyah.

Your ocean green eyes stood out amidst the dull brown eyes of the other children. You glanced up at me and narrowed your eyes, looking me up and down as if you were searching my soul to see if I was worthy. I looked at the other children who played with each other, laughing loudly. Faisal came to my side and put his arms behind his back. I ignored his arrival and looked at you, more intently. You sat alone in a corner, face looking down now. Something was different about you.

"What do you say, sahib?" Faisal asked, breaking my daze.

I looked at Faisal and before I said anything, I noticed how frail and weak the orphanage owner looked. He was of Peshawar descent. He wore a mildly dirty white shalwar along with rimmed glasses that had an annoying habit of sliding off his nose as it was a prisoner attempting to escape. He had a bushy white beard that had a few small stains on it which resulted from the little time to eat lunch. His cane rested against the grey wall and the children were now playing with it, knocking it over and acting like they had done some great deed.

I pointed toward you. You thought you were sly, didn't you? I saw you fidget once my index finger pointed toward your direction, your eyes shot up for a fleeting second, then back down to playing with the worn-down rug. Faisal smiled. He whistled and this time you stood. Your body was slim and slender with short hair and a pair of plain sandals on your feet. You walked over silently, eyes taking in everything except me. You finally approached Faisal and he put his hand on your shoulder, causing you to take a deep breath. It seemed you knew what was coming because, before I knew it, your face welcomed a smile, a grin slowly beginning to form on the crevices of your face. You looked down again.

"Fahad Jan, do you know why I have called you here? Do you know who this man is?"

I looked at your face for your reaction. You shook your head slightly and mumbled something, kicked a toy across the room, still looking down.

"His name is Faraz," Faisal continued, "And he has come here to take you away. He wishes to adopt you, Fahad Jan."

Your head shot up and you looked at me again, seemingly in awe. The children behind you were now watching. A couple had their hands on their head; a few were staring angrily, wishing someone would come and take them away. Believe me, if I could save all of these orphans from the trouble they would find themselves in, I would. But I don't think even that would be enough to atone for my sins.

I knelt down to look at you, really look at you and I swear to God, I saw my late wife Raiyah in your mesmerizing green pupils. You held your hand out slowly. I didn't take it at first: The chance I would be taking and the responsibility blew my mind—feeding you, nurturing you, providing you with the basic necessities of life.

But then I envisioned you growing up. You falling asleep in my lap as I read you yet another five-page story; you were sleeping without a lamp for the first time, no longer afraid of the alleged monsters lurking in your closet amidst your Nike apparel. You riding a bike, graduating high school, getting a career, marriage, it all came rushing at me and supplied with me a shot of adrenaline. It was then I knew. I had to take you. I had to.

Your hand was still out in the air, waiting for me to grab it and never let go. I hesitated no more. I took it in my hand, forever binding us together.

Faisal spoke, "His birthday is December 24. He'll be two."

You smiled when he told me the day you entered this world. You finally mustered up the courage to look up at me and say softly, as softly as one could ever speak.

"Salaam."

And so we go.

KARACHI, 1988

I was getting married to the most beautiful girl in town, Raiyah Pasha. She had long silky black hair that stood out against her perfectly fair skin. Her long eyelashes and sultry gait drove every man crazy. But I was the one who she had fallen for, my chest that she laid on, my eyes she stared into. I stood there, in front of the mirror that reflected my image back at me, my only tuxedo shining in the fluorescent light above, my nicely polished, black shoes gleaming. I heard a knock on the mahogany door behind me, causing it to unhinge slightly, revealing a tall, weary man.

"I am so very proud of you, Faraz Jan," said my father, pure joy etched on his face, eyes shining in happiness. I turned to see him, standing there with his hands behind his back, gazing at me. His old-fashioned shalwar appeared to be an angelic, pure sort of white. It was fitting, I suppose. He held his hand out, beckoning for me to leave the room and enter my future.

I followed his hand, and at the end of the hallway, I spotted my childhood friend waiting there for me—Kamal. He smiled at me, hands in his pockets. The moment seemed so surreal as I walked up to him and he embraced me, congratulating me. I thought I heard a slight sob. I looked over his shoulder and saw my mother; tears of happiness parading down her face as if they were running a marathon. I let go of him and patted his shoulder as if it would ease the tears now freely falling.

My mother walked toward me and smiled, tears still pouring. She told me how proud Waqas and she were, how proud they were to be my parents. I smiled sheepishly and thanked her. She escorted me to the front of the room where I sat in a bright red and gold chair, strangers surrounding me and clapping, and unfinished plates of biryani inhabiting the square tables in the dining hall.

I took a seat in the chair amongst murmurs in the crowd. I looked to my left, and Raiyah was on the other side as it is with every Pakistani marriage. She was receiving her vows. It was my turn to receive mine.

I remembered the night before, when I came to her house because she had called me. She was gone, the gold dupatta still sitting on the chair, a remnant of her beauty. I ran into the bathroom, hearing loud gasps and I opened the door. There she was, hands on either sides of the sink, head down, tears mixing with the running water.

She didn't see me at first. Wiping her tears with her sleeve, she sniffed and looked up slowly. She saw me in the mirror and gasped then covered her face. I took a step forward and asked, "What's wrong?"

She told me nothing was wrong. That I should go and that she doesn't want me to see her like this, that I didn't deserve it. I told her she was crazy.

"I'm just so happy, Faraz," she babbled, "But I'm scared at the same time." I came closer, eyebrow raised and put my arms around her and whispered, "Shh!" into her ear.

She closed her eyes, robbing the mirror of the good fortune that it had come across of being able to copy those magical green eyes. We stood like that for a while, her and I, until her tears came to a stop and she turned to face me, allowing a smile to flee her previous melancholy face. I smiled back and said, "Come on. Tomorrow will be fine. Relax. I love you so much."

"That's true," she sighed. "You cheered me up." I turned and shrugged my shoulders.

"However," I began, "If I go out there without you, there goes my reputation. Oh, Faraz can't handle his own wife. So do me this favor." I winked at her. "Consider it the dowry."

She laughed and I told her not to worry about it. I would see her tomorrow.

The imam appeared now with his full black beard and black sharwani and Quran in his hand, standing by my side, waiting to perform the vows. He looked at me inquisitively and narrowed his eyebrows, his eyes flicking up to steal a glance at the clock. I shifted uncomfortably and cleared my throat. The butterflies in my stomach were stronger than ever. It was suddenly very hot and I pulled at my tie. It dawned on me that I was about to start a whole new life; I, the writer, getting married to the hard-working, gorgeous, future doctor, Raiyah Pasha. There had been rumors. Oh yes, disapproval as well. Why had the doctor decided to get married to the aspiring author? Out of all the wealthy, American clothes wearing, intelligent suitors that showed up at the Pasha's household, she chose the storyteller. Parents shook their heads and her friends had bugged her about it, asking her if she was crazy. I had a firm belief it would work. I loved her and no stereotypes or sense of normalcy that was void from the relationship would change that.

The imam, who introduced himself as Ahmed, was now reciting verses from the Quran. The room had grown silent as everyone hung on to Ahmed's every word, their eyes transfixed upon the holiest book of them all. Inadvertently, I closed my eyes and began nodding my head slightly. It's true that I didn't understand the Arabic language, but the flow and the beautiful sounds the words make when they come together came over me like a wave of euphoria. It put me at rest. The imam was now speaking English.

"Faraz Ahmad, do you accept Raiyah Pasha as your *bheevi*, as your wife for the rest of your life?" I heard a touch of contempt in his voice, as if he didn't agree with what has happening and why Raiyah Pasha didn't marry his son, Ali, the future doctor who would be graduating from Harvard Medical soon enough. I ignored the thought and nodded, smiled at him.

"I do, *sahib*, I do. Yes."

He asked me two more times and I had the same answer each time.

Ahmed closed the Quran and set it down on a table. "Congratulations," he said dryly. "You are now married."

The imam tapped my shoulder and broke me from my daze. I looked up and Raiyah strolled in, accompanied by her relatives, head looking down but I could have sworn I saw a slight smile on her face. It seemed like it took an eternity for her to reach the chair next to me. Her sister Aisha helped her sit and Raiyah kept looking down, keeping her reputation honorable and following the customs of Pakistani marriage. I felt so thrilled in that moment as perfect strangers threw flowers on my head. I looked sideways and our eyes meant, her hypnotizing green eyes confronting my light hazel pupils. I knew it. I knew we were meant to be together.

———

The night flew by quickly. The vacant soda cans had turned into drained bottles of exquisite wine, courtesy of my father of course. The blaring music had been turned down; now old Bollywood show tunes leaked out of the bass speakers and flooded the romance filled atmosphere.

People were sitting around, drinking tea, looking like zombies. I looked down at Raiyah who was in my arms, sound asleep. I then glanced up at the clock. It was now 4:27 AM. Before I woke her, I took a second and marveled at how amazing she looked while sleeping. Her hair covered her face as if it didn't want to share the beauty of her eyes with the rest of the world, keeping them to itself. I nudged her gently and she stirred awake, eyes now revealed. "Let's go," I urged. "It's late."

She mumbled something incoherently and fluttered her eyes slowly and sent a smile my way that made me mirror her automatically. "Your teeth are so white," she muttered, as she got up. I laughed and helped her get on her feet, careful not to wake any of the old, bearded strangers around us. I reached in the left pocket of my black dress pants and picked out the keys to the Honda Civic my father gave for my eighteenth birthday.

He had taken me out to this incredible restaurant and told total strangers that I was going to be a famous writer and a great writer. They clapped and they cheered for me; I smiled sheepishly and muttered thanks where as my father encouraged me to take praise in my stride. He said it was the mark of a true man. We stayed there late until he told me to wait in the restaurant. He walked outside and was gone for a good five minutes. He then came back outside and beckoned me to come outside. I followed his hand walked out, causing the bell to ring above my head, a chime alerting the owner of the restaurant that there would be no more loud laughter disrupting other customers.

I breathed in the cool night air, the moon shining brightly above my head and causing the car in front of me to gleam in the light. My father handed me the keys and smiled lightly. "It's a bit old," he said, "It'll need some fixing up. A lot maybe; but it'll do."

My eyes welled up and not looking at him, I said, "Thank you, Baba." I repeated it over and over again, taking a step forward after each sentence. I opened the car door and felt the interior. Smooth. I drove my father home that night in my new car.

Raiyah shook me and I came back to the present. She winked and said, "I'll drive." I handed her the keys and we walked out slowly, holding hands, completely ready to start a new life.

—

CHICAGO, 1989

I sat at a table, rubbing my eyes wearily, papers scattered all over the rose cherry desk, countless pencils on top of them. The lamp was now dim and I had just finished the first chapter. There was a knock behind me and I said, "Come in."

Raiyah came strolling in, clad in her Winnie the Pooh pajamas, cup of tea clutched in both hands, "How's it coming?"

"Not good," I replied and she rubbed my shoulder and rested her chin on my other. We were quiet for a minute as I looked over the plot intently. She broke the silence, "Let's go to sleep now, Faraz."

I shook my head and looked at Raiyah who was still as beautiful as our wedding night. Her hair had seemed to thicken and caught the ember of the fire, shining even brighter. Those eyes though. Those eyes.

I sighed deeply and replied, "Alright. Remember, we have to go visit Baba tomorrow night."

She nodded and said, "I would never forget. You know that."

I gave away a slight chuckle and pushed away from the cluttered desk, turning off the lamp, shutting off my laptop. I turned in the chair and got up slowly, stretching and yawning.

Raiyah went upstairs and I followed her. The thought came into my mind without warning. I had spoken with Kamal about this a few nights ago. About the overwhelming joy he felt when he heard the first words, when he saw the first steps. As we entered the bedroom, I blurted out, "What do you think about having a baby?"

Raiyah stopped in her steps. She turned around slowly, frowning. "Now?" She asked, perplexed. "Let us . . . wait until we become more financially secure, Faraz. It won't be fair to our baby."

I wasn't listening. I found myself staring up at the ceiling, eyebrows raised inquisitively. "Kamal," I said.

She said, "Kamal can afford to have one right now, Faraz. Please understand."

I looked at her in disdain . . . but then I fell under the spell of her emerald eyes. I smiled and nodded. We got into bed. We watched TV for a while then we let our respective saviors take us away. Hers was sleep; mine, as always, was a book. As I lay propped up against the headrest with Salem's Lot resting on my rising and falling chest, I thought of what had happened in the past year. I had married a gorgeous girl; I had my father's blessing to come to America, where people would take me as a legitimate writer. Then a month later, Kamal's marriage to a girl named Jamila. She was short, petite. She had a cute little laugh that reminded me of birds chirping. Her cooking wasn't that bad either.

Then one day, resting on the balcony, I got a call from Pakistan. It was Kamal. He told me my father was sick. He had been sleeping, until he began shaking uncontrollably, froth leaking out violently from his mouth, his eyes rolling into the back of his head. Kamal told me he had sent Baba out on a flight here to Chicago. He had been acting strange after my mother's death but this frightened me to no end. When I picked him up from the airport, he was leaning onto a pitch black cane, staggering toward me, a smile forming slowly. Too slowly, I put his arm around my shoulder and took him to the conveyor belt to get his luggage. I placed it in the mini cart and exited the building. He had been quiet this entire time, watching me silently. I felt as if he were taking the sight of me as a grown man in. As if he would never see me again. In a sense he was drinking my appearance like an elixir. I blocked the thought out of my mind and promised myself to never think such a thing. I helped him enter the car he gave me over ten years ago and he said one word, "Still."

I laughed nervously and nodded. "Yes, Baba. Still." I took him straight to the hospital. He sat silently, eyes closed now. I gripped the steering wheel, clenching and unclenching. We approached the hospital in about twenty minutes. I helped him get out and took him straight to the emergency room. As I took his hand and guided him there, he mumbled something. I stopped and asked him to repeat. Silence was the only reply.

My father was never a firm believer in God. He wasn't very religious and enjoyed an alcoholic drink now and then. But lying there, on the pure white bed with wires attached to him, he recited the few verses he knew from the Quran, with pleads to Allah in between his prayers.

I spent the night with him, watching over him with careful eyes. I fell asleep soon. He would be fine, the doctors said the following morning. I thanked them gratefully and drove home. I was still gripping the steering wheel. Clenching and unclenching.

—

Noises; people bustling in and out of the house and shouts of a funeral and a tragedy filling the suddenly humid atmosphere.

I woke slowly, my eyes adjusting to the light. The room was a mess and I heard countless feet pounding the wooden floor downstairs. A feeling of fear invaded my heart and I suddenly felt very light headed. Before I lifted myself up from the bed, I saw Raiyah by my side, her hand clutching mine, applying tremendous pressure. Her mesmerizing eyes seemed worried. I think I knew then. In a little less than a year, Raiyah and I had learned how to communicate through eye contact. She started crying and threw herself at me as I cried as well, stroking her hair and looking up at the ceiling. I should have been there. It was entirely my fault. She was done now. She looked me in the eye, sniffed and told me the funeral would be tonight. I took a deep breath and nodded and we sat there for what seemed like an eternity, dealing with the first of many losses in our marriage.

—

Cars flooded the mosque in downtown Chicago. Horns blared throughout the area and Chicago police helped all the cars find their way into the parking lot. I sat inside, legs crossed, my hands together in front of my face, reciting the few prayers I knew. As I sat and prayed, more and more people entered the small room and each one came by and shook my hand with nothing but good things to say about Waqas Ahmad. Some I recognized from childhood when my father would have his little get-togethers in his study with his friends, and they would smoke until 2 AM, discussing politics, soccer, cricket, you name it. Others, I had never seen before. The prayers were held and the imamimam who I would go to for another reason years later began speaking loudly.

While he prayed, I wondered about the unfairness of the world. How death was the only constant in life, how it was inevitable, yet some of the stories I saw on the news . . . abductions, rapes, killings. It seemed as if the world was already going downhill and all the evil in the world was a great big snowball rolling down a hill in wintertime in Denver. As if it started as a small snowball, with maybe thievery or dishonesty. Then the crimes began piling up, like rolling down the snow-blanketed hill. Eevil—overwhelming me along with everybody else and there was nothing we can do about it. Evil will run its course. It's how we respond to it; that makes us who we are.

I woke from my daze and found everyone was leaving. Some grown men were in tears, their beards now moist, shaking my hand and leaving. I beat myself up mentally for not sobbing. Looking back now, I guess I was just in shock and still didn't believe he was truly, actually gone. I sniffed and stepped outside. Raiyah was there, talking to a group of women, when she saw me. She excused herself and ran up to me, hugging me.

I whispered in her ear, "I'm going to miss him." And I started weeping, weeping like I had never before, in my wife's arms, still wondering about the unfairness of the world.

2 months later . . .

The fan had whirred noisily above me as I first met Dr. Gregg. I sat across from him, leaning back in my chair, smiling. He was a typical Brooks Brothers, shaven head, deep baritone voice kind of guy. The light reflected on his bald head as he sat forward, putting the tips of his fingers together as he looked into my eyes. We talked for a bit then he started asking questions.

"So, Mr. Ahmad, what do you do?"

I shifted nervously and coughed. "I'm a writer."

The doctor's eyes lit up. "Is that so?" he asked. "I too always wanted to write something . . . you know what they say. Literature is the greatest form of communication and getting your ideas to countless people. It is quite amazing how much power a few written words can have on somebody."

I leaned forward now and asked, "Why didn't you write something then?"

The doctor laughed and said, "I'm lacking one vital ingredient."

My eyebrows rose.

"Talent," Dr. Gregg finished, smiling.

We both laughed then. Not knowing what the next few visits would bring.

Here, a month later, with the heat causing sweat to freefall down my forehead, he pulled out a file and his face suddenly became morose. Reminding me why I was here.

When he told me, I couldn't breathe. Someone had robbed me of my oxygen supply; someone had placed a pair of steel hands around my throat, cutting off my air.

He attempted to reassure me but I wouldn't hear it. My world was crashing down around me. I couldn't lose her. No. I just couldn't. A short while after losing my father; I just wouldn't accept it.

I stood suddenly, toppling the chair over, sending his files flying, littering the floor. He sat still, a worried yet unbelievably a calm expression on his face, as if he was used to it. I wanted to hit him. Hit him over and over again.

I was berserk. Hitting his plants over, causing the soil to color the maroon carpet an almost black, cracking windows. I didn't want to blame him. It wasn't his fault. He had helped me and hurt me at the same time. I didn't want to blame him; I had no one else to blame and God knows I had become sick and tired of blaming myself. Then I screamed. I screamed till my throat hurt and looked up at the heavens, asking why, what I have done to undergo such adversity, such sorrow.

Dr. Gregg was talking now; I wasn't listening. I was in my own world at that time, it was just me, alone and solitary in this cold world now, no one at my side and no one looking after me. I had no one else besides her. Kamal was off in Pakistan, living a happy life. Who was I to go to him about something like this? I heard him though; his attempts to console me flew over my head.

"Mr. Ahmad."

"God damn it."

"Please calm yourself."

"No, no, no."

I was now panting heavily, tears streaming freely. I looked up and he was quiet for a moment. He then stood up and said, "I am sorry. But it is God's will; I am merely sending it to you, Mr. Ahmad."

God's will; I refused to believe there was such a thing anymore. I glared at him, irate and he turned around, hands behind his back and pressed the button on an intercom system and told the nurse to escort me out of the office. A moment passed and an old lady opened the door and grabbed my arm. I yanked away, shooting her an angry look. Looking back at Dr. Gregg, I walked out of the room and headed outside and got into the car. Prepared myself to tell my wife she had breast cancer.

———

As I drove in my car, windows down, the wind gushing into the vehicle, drowning out the sounds of everyday life, I thought about a lot of things. There was so much sorrow in my life. Did I do anything to deserve it? My father once told me that perseverance was the key to success. But how much more should I persevere before I just break down and quit?

The phone rang. I took my right hand off the wheel and picked the phone up; looked at the caller ID. Kamal from Karachi. Hastily, I picked it up.

"Asalaam alaykum," Kamal greeted me. "How are you, Faraz?"

I took a deep breath. I was thankful for the fact that he couldn't see me because he would've known what I answered was a lie. "I'm good, Kamal. How are you?"

There was a pause. "Karachi is changing, Faraz. The only thing keeping me sane is my family. Ali spoke his first word yesterday—"Baba." I am so proud."

I felt a pang of jealousy.

Faraz?" Kamal continued, recognizing my silence. "I found a nice orphanage here. There's a boy I'd like you to meet. His name is Fahad—born just last week. He is in desperate need of a family. Someone just dropped him off at the door."

I wasn't listening. Raiyah was going to die and he was talking to me about moving on so soon?

He kept talking and I came in with sporadic "yeahs' yeahs" and "mhms". Then, as I was driving, a car crosses the red light and comes in my path. I cursed loudly and veered to the left, but it was too late. I got hit by the butt of the car and toppled over.

As I struggled to remain conscious, I heard Kamal yelling now through the phone. But I remembered then—the boy—the boy's name, Fahad.

I blacked out.

—

"Someone, get his pulse now!"; "Blood pressure 110 over 70!"; "I can't feel his pulse! Someone, check his neck!"; "Thirty-year-old Pakistani male, 180, 5"9', no biological family."

I couldn't breathe. I could hear what was going on around me but I couldn't do anything about it. No family? I had a family. I had Raiyah, I couldn't lose her, and she's the only thing I've got, no, no, no. I moved my left hand out and grabbed something; an arm.

Everything fell silent.

"What is your name, sir?"

I croaked, "Faraz Ahmad. What happened?"

"You were in a severe car crash. You'll be fine. It was quite an accident. Somebody up there must like you."

I turned away, fighting tears. The pain surged through my body. I thought my right arm was broken. My leg felt as if it were about to fall off.

"Raiyah?" I moaned.

There was a silence. Someone coughed. My heart skipped a beat.

"Where is my wife?" I demanded, forcefully now.

"In the hospital, Mr. Ahmad, with breast cancer. If you would like, I can arrange it so that your bed is right next to her."

I nodded slowly. Relief settled into my body, putting me at ease. I attempted to rise but I got pushed down

"Let's get you to the hospital, sir."

I suddenly felt very dizzy. Exhausted, I blacked out yet again.

—

The world knew of evil.

It knew the evil that encompassed the souls of serial killers, it knew the evil that pushed innocent teenagers into shooting up their schools, and it knew the evil that entered the dark hearts of demonic fiends such as Hitler or Stalin.

The world knew that Martin Luther King Jr. fought for a seemingly impossible cause and achieved at it; yet, at the height of one of the most important events of America, he was shot down simply because of the color of his skin. The world knew that Gandhi was a symbol of hope and he was simply doing the right thing yet his death came at the hands of one of the people he was trying to protect. And today the world knows that Barack Obama is not only changing politics, but is changing America and changing the world through his inspiring speeches, his plans for the nation and his myriad supporters. Obama has shown, time and time again, he will provide the best for America; yet, there are people in this nation hell-bent on assassinating him, not because they don't agree with his view on the Iraq war or his stance on the economy, no, not at all. Sometimes, all people see is color and ignore substantial, meaningful ideas. It's a pity, to be honest, that this election has brought the racists out of the grand doors of American society and has shown that Obama is wanted dead because he's black.

If all the people in the world that do good end up dead, then why bother? Why bother trying to inject a shot of purity into the world's figurative arm like a vaccine, when we all know that it will backfire? The world is becoming entrenched in this horrible thing and it's getting harder to simply decipher the difference between these two forces.

But you know what? You can still try. God willing, you can still try. Pick up that trash, open doors for people; just say hey to your coworker. If evil attempts to show its ugly face, you persevere. You get right back up and keep going because eventually, your efforts will become habits and evil will cower in fear.

Evil is a constant in everyone's lives, a force that lurks in the shadows of obscurity, ready to rain on your parade like a thunderhead. But if you can muster up the courage to fight against it, you have just accomplished something others never will.

As I lay there, in the wee hours of the morning, contemplating this in my mind, I tossed and turned in my bed, sweat building a thick sheen on my brow. I propped myself up on my elbows and turned to look at the clock. 3:21 AM. The room was deathly quiet, crickets chirping outside the glass windows, the moon shining its light into a specific spot on the floor.

I was fighting evil. I was cheating death; I knew I was going to live. The boy's name kept popping up in mind. Fahad. I wanted a child, I wanted for Raiyah and I to have a family, like the ones on TV, where everything turns out right and there is never stress or concern.

But this is real life. And what happened the next morning was very, very real.

—

Someone was pushing me, shoving me. I opened my eyes slowly and adjusted to the light above. There was lots of movement; nurses clad in white attire scurried in and out of the room. I looked around and saw they were around a bed. My heart skipped a beat. Raiyah.

I attempted to get up, to break free of these wires and see what was happening to my wife, my love, my everything. A doctor pushed me back down roughly, I pushed him away and attempted to get up again but they held me down, four men this time. I heard alarming tones enumerating medical terms, a machine on a rolling cart being wheeled over to the bed.

I was still trying to get up. Then I heard it. The sound that signals the end of life, no matter how short or long, how good or bad, the sound that tells one their time is over, that they have reached the limit of their time on Earth.

Lying there, I heard a single solitary beep, and a flat green line running horizontally across a pitch black screen. The medical staff backed away and I saw my wife, I saw her with her eyes closed and her chest not rising anymore.

I fell to my knees and wailed. What other choice did I have but to lament, and to grieve; to grovel at the feet of these doctors?

I was in love with Raiyah. I had never felt such a connection with anybody in my life, it was as if we could reach others minds effortlessly, we ended each other's sentences and so much more.

And now she was gone. Just like that. Gone to a disease out of my power, cause God knows I would do anything to keep her alive for one more second, one more minute, and one more day.

They helped me up and I pulled away again, tears streaming down my face. In that moment, I knew what I had to do.

I had to go to Pakistan.

—

Life was quiet after Raiyah passed away. I seldom smiled anymore, and ever since the funeral I've lost interest in things that fascinated me. TV seemed drab, food tasted like nothing; it was all a big bout of sorrow and grief. Kamal would call time to time and try to push me into taking the next flight to Pakistan.

I was scared though. I didn't want to put my heart out there again, and watch it be chopped to bits. As frail as it may make my soul seem, I was scared of being hurt again. I had the chance to have a family, to adopt this child and live out my dreams through him but based on past events when I was ambitious, they turned out miserably.

I was often alone in the house, working on plot ideas and character development for my first published work Gold & Silver, which was about an alchemist who traveled throughout the world, spreading his knowledge.

One day when I was finishing up a chapter, the doorbell rang. I sighed and rubbed my eyes. Got up and walked over to the door, opened it, and saw Raiyah's sister Aisha standing there.

Startled, my brain started racing. Aisha lived in New York, what was she doing here in Chicago? I hadn't seen her since the funeral a couple months ago and even then I couldn't bear to speak to her, not then, not ever, frankly. She was nothing like Raiyah. No one was.

I stared at her blankly until she asked, "Are you going to let me in?"

I snapped out of it and nodded. "Yeah, my bad." I stepped to the side and allowed her to enter the house. She strolled in, looking at the walls at all the photos of Raiyah and I.

I closed the door and asked quietly, "Any reason why you're here today?"

She turned around and said softly, "Faraz, I know you're upset. I know you're distraught and that you've been torn apart mentally time and time again, but she would have wanted you to be happy. She would have wanted you to move on."

I looked at her. Again, despite her kinship to Raiyah, I didn't find any similarities between the two. Raiyah was everything Aisha was not. I replied slowly, "What are you saying?"

Aisha sat in the chair and ran both hands through her hair. "I'm saying that all this moping and fussing isn't doing you any good. Come with me to New York. You can live with me and my family until you become confident enough to go out on your own."

I turned around and sat down. "I'm not leaving this house."

She sighed and told me I was making a mistake. Looking around the house and the disheveled papers, the dirty plates lying on the stained tables, she said, "Consider it. I am telling you, she really would have wanted you to move on."

I knew Raiyah Pasha more than anybody. That was what I believed, and I did so passionately. In my passion, I forgot that Raiyah grew up with Aisha, and they spent many days together, growing up with each other; Raiyah's father was, well, not much of a father and her mother had passed away when she was young.

"I can't leave. This house is all I remember her by" was my answer.

Aisha spread her arms out and looked at me incredulously. "You've become a mess! Look at the house! Clothes everywhere, unwashed dishes . . . You can't stop living, Faraz."

I got up from my chair and said a little loudly, "I didn't know you could be penalized for loving somebody nowadays. What is wrong with the world, Aisha, when I just lost my wife, and you're already here berating me?"

I turned around and said, "I'm packing now. I want you to leave."

Aisha's face lit up. "New York?" she asked hopefully.

Without looking back "No. Pakistan."

—

As I drove toward Chicago O'Hare International Airport, my confidence grew stronger. I was putting my hopes out there again, for the second time and for some reason, I felt reassured. I was at rest with myself and I had no premonition of getting my soul crushed or being disappointed again.

When I had called Kamal and told him I was on my way, he was ecstatic.

"Faraz, you'll be staying with me, you won't spend a single dollar, you need anything, just let me know and I'll get it. No worries, Bhai," he sputtered over the phone, repeated countless reassurances and telling me not to worry about a thing. He told me how excited he was for me to see his son Ali and his wife Jamila, his family, in other words.

It had been a year or so since I had been to Pakistan. Kamal told me it hadn't changed much, but I knew he always thought that I had been a tourist in my country; I just didn't know it.

I approached the bustling airport and parked my car in the lot, sighed and looked at the interior and got out of the car. There was no turning back now. I started walking, dodging the inhabitants of the smoking section in front of the entrance to the airport; the smell of smoke always seemed to mark a permanent stain on my soul like a defect.

The process, as always, was hectic. At that time, O'Hare International was the busiest airport in all of America. Hundreds of thousands flocked in and out every day with business meetings to attend, long-lost friends to reunite with, family to meet and much more. Airports can be real blessings, they can.

It took an hour or so to get through all the steps of the airport and I was sitting in gate E32, reading a book—as usual.

The flight would take me to Europe first, probably Copenhagen. From there, I would fly to Dubai and take a short flight to Karachi.

I checked my watch. 7:30 PM. Boarding wouldn't start for another thirty minutes. I yawned and leaned back, stretching my arms out.

What I figured was that, child or no child, it would be best for me to go to Pakistan for a while. To forget the rushed, tension-filled life here in Chicago, Illinois, and relax in Pakistan, where everyone was understanding and everyone knew everyone.

America was a place to mourn my past. Pakistan was a place to bury it.

———

I always disliked takeoffs. I don't know why, but paranoia and panic invaded me whenever planes took off from the ground. I recited a quick prayer I remembered from my childhood, closing my eyes and muttering it softly. I was gripping the armrest tight.

The takeoff this time, however, was smooth, and I was glad I recited my prayer. I took it as a good omen and my grip loosened on the armrest.

"A little tense?" asked the man next to me smiled and held his hand out. He had short blond hair and blue eyes as did the lady sitting next to him. He seemed friendly enough.

I laughed and shook it as I said, "Just a little."

"Aren't we all," he chuckled. "I'm visiting my son who lives in Copenhagen, and I'll be seeing him for the first time after four years . . . . Where are you headed to? The name's Chris, by the way." "My wife, Michelle," he gestured to the seat next to him.

"Faraz," I said. "That's great. I'm actually headed back home to Pakistan. Sometimes you need a little break, you know?"

Chris smiled and said, "I know what you mean. Life here isn't the most peaceful. Sometimes you just want to get home to your family."

I cringed, but he didn't notice.

He continued, "Sorry to trouble you, but are you Faraz Ahmad?"

My eyebrows rose. I backed up a little and said, "Yeah . . ."

"Faraz Ahmad . . . an honor to meet you. Your book is very touching." The man pulled out a paperback copy out from his backpack and showed it to me.

I started laughing out of relief. "Thanks," I replied sheepishly.

"Don't mention it. I read it in a week. I just couldn't drop it. My son requested it and he rarely reads."

I grinned again, partly proud, partly embarrassed. "Thanks," I repeated.

Chris placed the book back in the bag and said, "How long will you be in Pakistan?"

I fidgeted in my seat. I really wanted to go to sleep. "I'm not sure," I replied slowly: "Maybe for a while."

Both were quiet for a second, then Chris's wife pulled the book back out of the bag and handed it to me.

"Show it to your family. I'm sure they would be extremely proud," Chris told me.

"Your wife is so lucky to have such a great husband," Michelle added.

I was quiet again. "But . . . your son?"

Chris assured me, "I'll buy him another copy when we get there. You've earned it, Mr. Ahmad. You're an honorable man."

I took the book and got up abruptly and said I was going to the bathroom. Instead, I asked the flight attendant for a seat change.

I got one next to the window and stared out at the clouds and wondered when I would no longer feel pain like this.

———

"Say salaam, Ali. Say salaam to Faraz uncle."

The boy smirked mischievously and held his hand out while still looking down. I grinned and shook his small hand up and down.

"A salaam alaykum. May Allah's blessings be upon you."

I repeated the religious salutation and took my shoes off at the door—walked in and looked around the neat house. I had this impression they panicked to tidy up right before I arrived.

The curtains were drab; they were spread apart so you could see some of the town. The carpet had a few stains on it and the ceiling was white as can be.

"It has been such a long time," I heard a voice behind me say.

I turned and saw Kamal with Ali in his arms and Jamila at his side. I smiled. They looked so happy together, just as a family should. Inadvertently, I envisioned Raiyah, and I with a family.

Jamila asked, "Where's Raiyah?"

I looked down and realized I hadn't told them. I sniffed and coughed and then said quietly, "She passed away about a month ago. Cancer."

There was a tension-filled atmosphere, and Ali nudged closer to his father. I don't think he's ever seen a grown man cry like I did.

I took a deep breath and Jamila broke the silence.

"Dinner is ready," she chirped.

She hurried into the kitchen, swinging her white dupatta, her white scarf, over her shoulder as she prepared to bring the food out onto the dining table.

Kamal began: "What happened? I am extremely sorry, Faraz Jan. Such things shouldn't happen to good people."

I shrugged. "Breast cancer," I said. "Unexpected . . ."

Kamal asked for a moment of silence to pray. Ali and him both held their hands up as did I.

"Allah, the most merciful, the most beneficent! Please allow the lovely woman Raiyah Pasha into heaven, for she has had a life cut short and never did anyone harm. Ameen!" he finished, sighing.

"Ameen," I repeated mindlessly, her green eyes flashing in my mind. They never went away, they did.

Jamila brought in the food and placed it on the table and followed with napkins. I ate eagerly—airline food isn't always the best.

When we finished, Kamal told me he was taking me out.

When I asked where, he told me he's taking me to the orphanage where my life changed forever.

As we headed out the door, a myriad of thoughts swarmed my mind. I missed Raiyah more than anything at this one moment. I saw her in my dreams, every single night, yet we never had a chance to talk. Her first question would always be about our child, how he was doing.

I would sigh and tell her I haven't adopted yet. She'd say oh! and stand awkwardly. God, I hated it. I hated that she was so concerned about the child. I was selfish, I know.

But that night, after meeting the child and talking him to sleep, I dreamt of her again. But she didn't ask any questions. Not one. All she did was smile, a smile as shiny as the sun, eyes as green as the grass, and she just stood there, smiling.

—

CHICAGO, 1995

"Fahad! Get up! The bus is waiting for you outside!"

You put on your Chicago Bulls jersey to compliment your black basketball shorts and Jordans with your untidy black hair interrupting your vision through your emerald eyes, yawned and looked out the window. A classic, long, yellow bus with children filing in, ready for their very first day of school.

I knocked on the door sharply and said, "Fahad, hurry, the bus will leave without you!"

I heard your feet shuffle across the floor, and I smiled again. I had been smiling ever since that trip to the orphanage. The door swung open and there you were, putting on your backpack and shoving your hands in your pockets. I took your hand and we both walked outside in the cold. We finally approached the bus and you turned and looked at me.

"I love you Baba."

I smiled and it took me a moment for me to say that I loved you back. You grinned big and ran onto the bus, high-fiving the bus driver and asking what her name was.

"First day, huh?"

I looked to my left and saw another mom. She had long, dark hair and a scarf around her neck with a big jacket and complete with gloves.

"Yeah," I said, watching the bus take off.

"It's tough watching them go, isn't it? You feel as if they're not ready yet, that they could use just one more day at home."

I was quiet.

She held her hand out. "By the way, my name is Ridah."

I shook it firmly. "Faraz."

She pointed down the street with her long arm. "I live just a few houses down from here; just me and my son Faizan."

I smiled politely and pointed my thumb behind me. "The bus comes right in front of my house here."

She grinned. "What's your son's name?"

I paused, my son. "His name, his name is Fahad. Fahad is my son."

Her eyes lit up. "Oh, was he the little guy with the Jordan jersey? He was so cute!"

"Yeah," I laughed. "Jordan is his idol. He wants to play in the NBA when he grows up."

"Doesn't every kid?"

We both laughed.

Then, out of nowhere, it just slipped out of my mouth. I beat myself up mentally for saying it, I felt like I had just slapped Raiyah in the face but it had been such a long time . . .

"Hey, it's getting kind of cold out here . . . . You wanna come inside? I could make some tea."

She seemed surprised. Then she smiled again. "Sure. I'd like that."

I smiled thinly and we walked into the house.

—

"A writer?! Really? That's incredible!"

The fireplace was crackling, adding a sort of soundtrack to our discussion. Ridah had hoisted herself up on the leather chair, clutching the cup of tea and taking sporadic sips, eyes always on me.

I was leaning back in the recliner, sipping on a coke and said, "Yeah, I have a few copies lying around somewhere. I'll get them for you."

She grinned and said that was fine.

I asked about her son Faizan—how he was, what shows he liked, and if Fahad and him could become good friends. She took a deep breath and said, "Faizan's been going through some tough times recently. My, uh . . . my husband ran away when I was pregnant with him. Lately, the child's been coming home with stories of how the kids tease him."

I shifted uncomfortably and replied, "That must be awful . . . I dread the day when Fahad will ask about his mother."

Ridah pointed to a photograph to one of our wedding pictures, resting against the wall on the counter, gleaming in the overhead fluorescent lights. "Is this your wife?"

I swallowed and looked down at the floor, fiddling with the tea cup. "Yes. She passed away a while ago—cancer."

For some reason, I felt ashamed talking about it to this perfect stranger. I felt the need that I was supposed to be strong and not fall into a state of sadness. I looked up to face her and I said, more firmly, "Her name was Raiyah. She meant the world to me."

"It must have been a terrible loss . . ."

That's when I realized that, if I was talking to any other person, they wouldn't be able to relate. But Ridah's former husband was out there somewhere, wherever he was, the point is that he's not at her house, raising his son, bringing in income, just being there for Faizan. There's something called personal accountability, something in which I always believed in and always will, and it led me to believe that it was my responsibility to raise Fahad in such a way that he would never regret a thing like I have done countless times in life. I had to raise him in a way that would never put me in a situation that I have to apologize for him, but more importantly, a situation that would never let him apologize for himself.

We talked for a little more and, hating myself for it, I was enjoying myself. We had many things in common such as favorite books, same hobbies and laughed frequently at old jokes we had heard in our childhood growing up in Pakistan. We ended up getting in the car and driving around to get a bite to eat. She always ordered a cup of tea at the end of her meal, always with two tablespoons of sugar and this—this she never forgot. As we ate at the local Starbucks, I asked her more about herself. She was actually a teacher at the local high school and said she had a passion for teaching children. I admired that and we got so caught up in our conversation that we forgot the time. Laughing, we threw everything away and sped back to the house with the windows down.

As we approached the house, we saw the classic yellow bus pulled up right in front of the driveway. You came out first, looking around. You looked genuinely happy and you were smiling wide. An older child came out behind him with a smirk on his face. Ridah's face lit up and laughed, "There's my little third grader!"

No sooner had the words come out her mouth than he was pushed down into the sidewalk, crying out as he fell and your backpack's items spilling onto the road. I was startled; I couldn't function for a second. Then I looked up and saw Faizan standing before you, grinning and laughing with a group of his friends as they teased him. I got out of the car and helped him up as he started laughing even more at the sight of me.

Faizan snickered, "Ah, so little 'Fahds' can't defend himself, eh? Gotta bring his old man to save him."

I was about to say something but you beat me to it. "Shut up! I didn't do anything to you!"

His grin faltered and his eyes narrowed, observing me and him. He took a step closer and said, "I wonder why fathers are treated like royalty. Maybe it's because that's all you have. You're just an orphan that got lucky; don't try to kid yourself that you're not."

Suddenly, I realized I was seeing, for the first time, American bullying. A throng of kids were now standing behind Faizan, jeering and laughing. I realized this was the way that these children made friends; by making themselves, no, by trying to make themselves look better by making others look worse.

You looked up to me and hugged me around the waist. Ridah had parked the car and had come out with a glare that would have caused the devil himself to apologize. Faizan saw her coming and, suddenly, got on his knees in front of you and begged for forgiveness. It was convincing too—but not enough—I turned toward the house and walked inside, making sure you got in the house before I did.

—

KARACHI, 1987

The wind was singing its song, the autumn leaves adding color to the soundtrack as the wind carried them throughout the air. I sat at a bench, checking the time constantly. I was meeting Raiyah Pasha here. It was a secret place, one I always remembered. It was here where I had kissed her for the very first time as she sat on this very same bench, her glasses resting on the tip of her nose as she read a book.

"Put that book down and give me a kiss," I remember saying.

The moon was shining brightly now and I heard a faint rustle behind me.

I have known Raiyah for a long time. We were good friends for a while. She had caught my eye at the dinner parties my father hosted and we always met up in secret behind the house, reveling our moment together yet scared as hell we would get caught by some frantic aunty or some lunatic of an uncle. The fear made it that much more exciting. I remember how her hair was so soft to the touch, how it overtook me, the scent of it. But those eyes had captivated me. I swear, every time I closed my eyes, I would see hers. Those green eyes made me feel like I was falling and falling into her pupils and I never wanted to hit the ground.

She approached me and remarked, "You smoke, huh . . . ."

Grinning, I crushed out the cigarette into the ashtray beside me. "Just recently—not a big deal."

She laughed, although not fully sure. Her eyes rested upon the smoldering cigarette, watching the remainder go up into the air.

"Is it because of that new crowd you hang around with, Rozzy?"

I smiled when she said my name. "They're just some new friends, Ray. And besides . . . the ladies think it's sexy."

Her eyebrows shot up at this as I knew they would. She got a little closer to me on the bench and said, "It's not sexy, trust me. And tell me who these girls are."

I lit another one—blew smoke out. "Oh, you know."

"Know what?"

"That they're nothing compared to you."

I saw her blush immensely despite her feeble attempts to hide it. She asked, "Why did you call me here, Faraz?"

I grinned at her and stood up. Dropped the second cigarette on the ground and crushed it with my foot as I took her hands in mine. We were the only people in the park, the leaves blowing around and the stars shining bright, as if they were envious of us.

"I love you Raiyah. You mean the world to me. I can't . . . I can't imagine life without you; only with you. When I met you . . . it was like a dream."

Raiyah was now crying. I took my thumb to wipe her tears away and said, "Come with me. There's something I want you to see."

She took a deep breath and hugged me tight. Her head against my chest, she whispered, "This is where you kissed me, isn't it?"

I nodded and replied, "You remember."

"How couldn't I?" she whispered.

I pulled her away from me and told her to turn around. "Look at the sky," I whispered into her ear.

It had taken a large sum of money. My father helped with the price; he paid about three fourths of the cost. It took days to plan.

But it was worth it. Fireworks shot up in the sky, illuminating the nightline, illuminating her face.

In red, across the night sky, was a marriage proposal.

She was crying even more now. "I accept!" She kept yelling it over and over again. "I accept, Faraz, I accept!"

I took her hand and we ran through the park, as if we were trying to reach those words embedded in the sky. The wind blew in our face—the laughs, the tears, the "I love you's"—I had never felt more at peace with anybody in my lifetime.

We kept running throughout the park, the wind blowing her tears away, and I swear the stars shone a little brighter.

—

1997

You loved music.

I would never see you without the toy guitar in your hand, rocking out around the house, begging me to play the drums for you on the trash cans. Your teachers would send notes home stating that you would start tapping the desks with your pencil frequently during class.

You were a smart kid, though. You knew what your priorities were. You wouldn't touch the toys before you finished all you had to do and tell me about your day. Sometimes, you would even try to read my work and tell me if it was good or not. I'd watch you out of the corner of my eye as you sat crisscross, eyebrows furrowed, obvious that you were having difficulty in deciphering my words. However, you wouldn't say a bad thing—never.

"Good job, Baba! I really liked it!" That was always your response and it felt so much more valuable coming from you than it did from the *Chicago Tribune* or the *New York Times*.

We had settled down now. Routines were established, rules were made; everything went smoothly in the house. Occasionally, I'd catch you staring at a photo of Raiyah and tracing her face with your fingers. When I saw you like this, I immediately felt like a fake, a phony. My heart bled for you, the harsh realization that you could not have a mother to be there for you hit me hard. I knew Raiyah would have loved you. She would taken everything about you into her hands and tell me not to worry a thing. I felt like the biggest phony sometimes when I tried to comfort you, knowing Raiyah would embarrass my efforts without even trying.

The day you asked about her was a day I'll never forget. By then, foolishly, I had assumed that there was a general acceptance, a general knowledge of the situation. One day, I was drinking some tea and watching the news when you came up to me in tears, your eyes puffy and red.

I had turned off the TV and asked you what the matter was. You sniffed and held up a broken photograph of me and Raiyah.

You told me it was show and tell day at school today, and that you had taken this photo to school to show all your friends. And then you had encountered Faizan after school.

The look of this kid; if Donkey Kong ever had a child, Fahad and I had found him. He was medium height yet wide, always eating something and an arrogant jeer always gracing his puffy face. After he'd do what he came to do, he'd yell, "Smell ya later!" even though he'd be smelling nobody but himself on the way back home. It was a mix of sweat and candy, 24/7. Faizan didn't believe in napkins either; he just used his right hand.

Ridah was great, don't get me wrong. I had found solace in her; she was like my sister. We had reached a mutual agreement though, to keep our sons away from each other. However, what happens at school is beyond our control.

You showed me the broken photograph and torn picture and my eyes welled up. I was angry. I was irate, disappointed, torn apart . . . you can't imagine, Fahad, you just can't. And then you said, "Why do you care so much, Baba? Who is she?"

I looked at you for a second, observing your face. Your eyebrows were relaxed and you stood patiently, waiting for my answer.

It was a simple question about an extraordinary woman.

"Come here," I beckoned. You jumped into my lap and looked up at me.

I sniffed and said, "I am going to tell you everything about this person. Do you understand, Fahad?"

You didn't understand, even several years later when I showed up to your house. You didn't understand the connection I had with her; no one did. It was magical. But at that time, seven years old, you did what I expected you to do; smile and nod.

I sighed, sipped a cup of tea, leaned against the wall and spoke:

—

"I was twelve years old. Sweating profusely, I looked at Kamal next to me who had remained adamant in fasting despite the hot sun and the countless hours of cricket. He was looking up at the sky, eyes squinting as he rambled on and on about something. I wasn't really listening; my eyes were focused on an old broken-down jeep that had pulled up outside my house."

"A young girl had stepped out of the back seat, her long, black hair falling down her back. I was mesmerized. And that was before I saw her eyes,

Fahad. She had these emerald green eyes, just like yours. You have her eyes. I might be embarrassing with you with all this talk but please, you wanted to know, so I'm telling you."

"Oy, Kamal," I said, squinting in the daylight. "Who's that girl?"

He smiled. "That, my friend, is a girl out of your league. Come, we have another game to play."

I didn't pay any attention to him and said, "Kamal, she's going inside my house."

"To your house!" Kamal put his hands on his cheeks and set his mouth agape in feigned surprise. "She might as well be your soulmate!" He chucked a rock on the road and continued, "Four eyes Parveen visited mine the other day with her whale of a mother, and you don't see us going crazy."

She walked toward the house with my parents and as my father opened the door, I heard him whistle, scanning the horizon for me. I put the cricket bat down and told Kamal I had to go. He yelled after me but I took off running, curious as to who this girl was.

Thoughts ran through my mind. Those eyes had captivated me. Who was she? I wondered. As I walked into the house, I saw her sitting on the sofa, looking bored as her father laughed at a joke with my father.

I didn't want to attract any attention. Not yet. I was just about to go into another room when my father commanded, "Faraz. Come here, I want you to meet somebody." I winced.

Halfway to freedom, one foot through the door and my father pulled me back again.

I put on a smile and entered the living room, shaking the girl's father's hand, said my salaam. As I sat down, I caught the girl looking at me.

My father began, "This is my son Faraz. Faraz, this is Abbas Uncle and his daughter, Raiyah."

I looked around the room and spotted my mother preparing several dishes and muttering to herself, debating which ones to actually serve. She was the biggest overachiever, Fahad. She would cook for a whole day when she caught wind of guests coming over. She'd cook a lot of food and then put out the ones that were the best and then would walk down to the local mosque and donate the food. However, while preparing the food, she would be standing with another woman who would be insisting on helping and who my mother would silence and tell her to stop being ridiculous.

That's when I realized there was no other woman there with my mother, no Mom there with Raiyah, there was no wife there with Abbas uncle. Curious, my eyebrows narrowed. I had never seen an incomplete family and the thought killed me. I had no idea I would have an incomplete family of my own when I grew older. Thank God, I have you though, Fahad, thank God.

Abbas was laconic in his speech toward her; when they spoke, his words consisted of grunts and one word commands for more bread, more water, insisting that my parents should not trouble themselves, his daughter will get it.

As she stood to fill a water pitcher and her bare feet hit the kitchen floor, she scanned the room, as if she was trying to find a way out, a way out of the darkness and into the light.

That's what most people spend their life doing, Fahad. Some people stay stuck in the dark for only a short while others spend eternity in the shadows of obscurity, praying, hoping for a light that will never come.

It's a pity that such things happen in the world, but what can we do? As my father always told me, one who spends his life looking for the light will never realize it was right in front of them.

Raiyah Pasha's light was right in front of her as well.

Our eyes locked as she picked up the cold water pitcher, pouring it into different cups, her green eyes still on me.

"Faraz. Faraz."

Disrupted from my gaze, I looked to the source of the noise; my father.

"Faraz, could you please go upstairs now?"

It was then I realized I had been looking at Raiyah for much, much longer then necessary. Abbas was staring at me with an icy, cold glare, neither warm nor inviting. Silently, I crept up the stairs, turning my back to and plunging Raiyah back into darkness.

—

I sat on the bed, clutching either side as I heard the jovial laughter and the clinking of my mother's expensive china downstairs. I wondered if they would be here longer yet I was frightened to go down the stairs. Feeling a sudden urge to go to the bathroom, I got up and walked out the door. Took a right and was face to face with Raiyah.

"Hey," she said tentatively, eying me carefully, "where's the bathroom?"

I was silent. I couldn't talk; I was too busy taking the sight of her in; her long, black hair, her smooth and light complexion.

They say one's eyes are windows to the soul. Raiyah's emerald green eyes pierced my soul and seemed to dissect it, piece by piece. She stood, leaning toward one side, tucking her hair behind her ear, waiting for my answer.

"I'm Faraz," I finished lamely.

She laughed and said, "I'm Raiyah."

Again, I was speechless. She asked, again, "So where's the restroom?"

I pointed to the end of the hall. She thanked me and walked past me, leaving a scent in the air that might have belonged to the most beautiful flower.

I didn't know it, Fahad, but I had already fallen for your mother.

I took a pause from telling the story and looked at you. You were captivated, looking up at me in awe, following my every word. You now believed that Raiyah was your biological mother and me your father. How could I crush your heart? How could I tell you your parents were most likely dead and that you were an adopted orphan? I just couldn't.

Throughout the many years of my kinship with you, I never revealed to you that we were not related. I couldn't let you lose that, because it's all you ever really had. You had been dropped off at a random orphanage in Karachi, as if you were a mere afterthought, something not to spend too much time thinking about. It led me to wondering how anybody could not accept the consequences of their actions, how anybody could not accept responsibility. I wept when I first thought it, I admit it. What could I do? I'm not exactly the most righteous person in the world but there are boundaries. Taking care of a life you helped conceive is one of them. I knew in my heart if I revealed the truth to you, it would break you. It would break your soul and leave me there to pick up the pieces.

There are cowards in this world and there are the brave. I wasn't either, yet I felt like I was finally doing something right. They say guilt leads to true redemption, Fahad, and this is something both you and I will eventually understand.

I didn't see her for a while after that day. Her face remained in my mind, all day, everyday yet I couldn't raise the punishable question of: Baba is Abbas uncle visiting soon? He would realize my motives instantly and scold me, scold me about not focusing on school work, how there would be time for girls later.

You are very lucky, Fahad, to grow up in such a modernized country in this day and age. You will possess things I never had or even dreamed of. It angered me and satisfied me at the same time. You would go on and be more successful than I ever was. Sometimes, I wondered what would happen if I grew up in such a country. Maybe I wouldn't be stuck writing for a living. Maybe I would have had a real "career" like an engineer or a lawyer. Or maybe I could become a doctor like my father always wanted me to be. College came, Fahad, high school ended and all my friends were applying to medical school, their hopes and aspirations originating from years of constant pressure of the idea that anything less was a failure. I was berated by all of them, the uncles whispering how I was foolish or naïve not to follow my father's footsteps like every single one of my peers.

But I felt proud in the end, proud that I was different from the rest of the crowd, proud that I strayed away from the standards of the Pakistani society I was raised in. I've made a decision, Fahad. You make a dream and you stick with it. You don't let anybody tell you otherwise. The word "no" doesn't exist in your dictionary.

I'm going to back you up in whatever dream you conjure up. You say you want to be a firefighter, I'll back you one hundred percent and never let up. You change your mind, the next day you want to be a teacher, I'm fine with that too. The point isn't your profession, Fahad. The most important thing in life is that you are happy with your choices, that you are content with them.

I saw Raiyah sporadically over the next two years. She would recognize me and wave or smile but we never got a chance to really talk yet just a smile set the butterflies in my stomach loose.

It all changed three years later at a wedding. We were both seventeen, dreams of America occupying our free time and looking forward to the day when we left the comfort of our homes and ventured out into the world.

She was taller now, more defined. Her jet black hair fell elegantly over her back, her eyes greener than ever. I found myself hoping that she remembered me, that while she scanned the crowd looking for her friends, her eyes would lit up as she spotted me amidst the throng.

I was sitting with Kamal and one of his other friends; both were chatting incessantly about school and cricket. I ignored them for the most part; my eyes were focused on her.

Kamal tapped on me on the shoulder. My gaze lingered in her direction for a second and then I looked at Kamal, semi angry at the disruption.

"Raiyah?"

"Nobody," was my answer.

My friendship with Kamal had become a difficult one. We were the best of friends, he lived right next door to me, our dads met up often; yet, I didn't feel as close to him as he did to me. I never told him the full story of anything, I would leave out bits and pieces of detail that I was sure he would find repulsive or vulgar.

Kamal had become a pure kid, he prayed five times a day, he fasted all thirty days of Ramadan and yet he still hung around me and didn't tell when

I sneaked in a samosa during fasting or when I didn't pay attention during prayer, my eyes diverting to the birds outside the window. After all these years, I felt bad that I hadn't treated others the way they treated me, Fahad, and it is this that will come back to haunt you. Believe me. It's a cliché you will hear many, many times in life, but remember this if you remember nothing else, Fahad. Treat others how you wish to be treated.

He introduced me to his friend Arjun, the son of the local doctor. I smiled and shook his hand as he nodded back at me. I looked back in Raiyah's direction, but she was gone. My hopes plummeted.

"I'm going outside," I told Kamal. "Gonna get some fresh air."

He nodded and told me to come back quick.

I waved him off and walked outside, hands in my pockets, preparing to embrace the icy October air, the wind blowing in my face.

It hits me as I step outside, the moon illuminating parts of the sidewalk. I glance around to make sure no one's looking and then light a cigarette and start smoking.

After a couple of puffs, I heard a sobbing noise behind me. It was faint and muffled, but I heard it. I walked to my left and spotted a young girl on the bench, hand in her face, crying her heart out.

Stamping out the cigarette with my foot, I approached the girl and she looked up, tears falling down her cheeks and I felt a pang of sorrow in my heart as I laid my eyes upon Raiyah.

"What happened?"

She looked up with her now red eyes; she had been weeping for a while.

"What do you want?" she sputtered, eyebrows narrowed. I stepped closer and, instinctively, wiped a tear away.

"I'm Faraz. Faraz Ahmad. Remember?"

She looked up again and replied, "I remember you. Now, what do you want?"

I sat down next to her, my heart beating fast, sweat already forming on my brow.

This was it; the real, true first impression. What should I have done? Asked questions? Simply comforted her with words? Let her have her space?

In the end, I made a decision that sealed our fate; that bound our lives together. I began talking.

She was bawling. Bawling about how life was unfair and how guys are stupid and how her father doesn't give a damn about her and how she misses her mother and on and on. Fahad, I pray to God you never witness the crying of a woman; it is one of those things that just tears your heart open. She wept to me, she confided to me, spilled some secrets that I never thought would be hidden by a girl like her.

She said she was sick of keeping all her emotions bottled up. Time and time again, she risks severe punishment and harsh rumors circulating throughout the community by sneaking out in the late hours of the night to meet up with boys who didn't care one bit about her or to go have a cigarette in some dark alleyway, scared that she'd get caught, fearing the consequences.

She looked up at me, eyes even more red and asked me, "Why are you doing this?"

It was then that it struck me just how far kindness can go. The boys her age only berated her, only used her once and then forgot about her. No one in her life had ever been as kind as I was to her that night, Fahad, and I want you to remember that kindness, ultimately, leads to the purest form of happiness. It still struck me as unimaginable that she not experienced kindness or sympathy like that ever before. My heart bled for her, Fahad, as it bleeds for you.

It's true I had no answer to her question. I just stared into her eyes and told her everything would be ok, that everything would be fine. She grabbed me and pulled me close.

"Thank you, Faraz," she wept incessantly, "God bless you."

———

Two years later, we were inseparable.

She called me her best friend, her soul mate, her everything. She was full of life yet closer to death than anyone I've known. She had intelligence and wit beyond her nineteen years and when it was just us beneath the stars, talking about the future, no, our future, we felt like we would always be together. She was incredibly brilliant yet humble, quiet, kind. I sat privileged but breaking inside as she shares her story. Her life has been so dark yet she possess undying optimism, the perpetual hope that better times will come, they have to, for God couldn't let her live like she had. God couldn't treat her badly from now on; he couldn't give her more misfortune after the death of her mother, after a father that could hardly be called one. She knew all this and yet preserved and stayed strong. Whenever we went out, women stopped her on the street and complimented her on her dress or her hair or a simple remark about how beautiful she was. I think it was God's way of telling her how sorry he was for the mess he put her in.

We were in love. She told me how I was different, how she was lucky to have me. But I knew the truth, Fahad. It was the other way around. When I was out with friends, they would always comment on her. Telling me how lucky I was, how they were jealous. The more time I spent with her, the more I became more relaxed, the more I took her for granted and that's one of my biggest regrets . . . God knows I have too many.

I recall New Year's Eve with her. It was magical, just me and her, counting down while looking for our fate in the stars. It was the first time I hinted at marriage, actually, yet she didn't hear me. She was busy looking in awe at the myriad of stars in the night sky, the cold breeze sweeping us over. I realized she wanted to savor the moment so I lay back and closed my eyes, hoping we'd be this way forever. Not many things in this life are perfect, Fahad, but that night was damn close.

Around 1 AM, I figured we should go home. We hopped in the car and drove around, the windows down, the city in celebration. But I'll never forget what happened once I pulled up to her house.

We approached the house and I came to a stop. Grabbed her hand and looked into her eyes.

"Tonight was amazing, Faraz," she said.

I was about to reply when I heard a tapping on her window. I looked past her and saw the giant of a man, Abbas Pasha, eyes irate and big. He swung open the car door, and grabbed Raiyah's arm; pulled her out of the car. I parked and jumped out, confronted him.

He got in my face and spat, "Who do you think you are? Some sort of sultan, some sort of prince? Why you're wasting your time with this . . . this girl, I don't understand. She's worthless."

I stood there and watched Raiyah take it. Take it like she had for her entire life. I watched her eyes well up for a second and then recover. My heart broke. His arm was still firmly clamped on her arm, despite her protests. He shoved her into the house and walked in after her and beckoned me with his index finger.

He was drinking a cup of tea, slowly, eyes on me, eyebrows furrowed. Raiyah sat next to him, tentatively, stealing glances at me when she could.

"What's your deal, boy? Have you no decency? The entire town talks of you and the girl, storming through the city in the late hours of the night. Imagine when your father hears them."

It irked me how he referred to his daughter as "the girl" and didn't once look at her. It made me want to hit him. I secretly made a vow I would never disrespect any girl like that.

"I don't know why I keep her around, to be honest with you," Abbas confessed, leaning back, legs splayed. "All she does is whine and moan and cook food fit for rodents. A waste of space, Faraz, is what you're in love with. Poor girl talks about going to America to study when she can't even find her way around this house. Tell me, is this your doing? Have you convinced her that the brash savior America is her ticket to a better life? God help me if she ever leaves Pakistan, she's staying right here."

I blurted out, "It was her idea, Abbas uncle. She's a smart girl, if you take the time to listen and talk to—"

He roared with laugher. Smashing his tea cup on the ground, he scoffed, "Wah wah! A smart girl, you say? She doesn't know what's going on in her own house because she's always with you. All she knows is you, Faraz. Pieces of paper with your name on it, pictures scattered throughout the house."

She stood abruptly and yelled.

"I hate you!" she bellowed, spitting in his face. "Why didn't you die instead of mom? It's not fair that I have to deal with your bullshit and all this drama you cause! I wish you were dead, you know that? I wish you were dead!"

I was flustered. It was all happening so fast; my mind was racing. She ran upstairs and shut the door. I still heard her sobbing.

Abbas and I sat in the room alone now. The shattered fragments of the tea cup glistened under the light. It was almost 2 in the morning.

"She never loved me as much as she does you, Faraz," he said quietly as he stared at the ground.

"Have you given her reason to?" I asked. He looked to the side, out the window. The night was still and a slight drizzle began to fall from the sky, battering the glass panes.

"I guess not," he finally said. "She doesn't know the full story, though, believe me."

I raised an eyebrow. "What story?"

He looked at me. I could tell the man had been through a lot; his eyes were full of pain and misery as if he had suffered through more than enough gloom in his life. The wrinkles on his face seemed more profound now as if someone had taken a knife and carved the lines in his face.

"I haven't been a good father, have I?" he asked me. I didn't say anything . . . I had a feeling he knew the answer.

"I loved my wife Faraz. As you know, she passed away during Raiyah's childhood. Do you know how she died, Faraz?"

I was quiet again but I could see where he was going. I didn't want to hear it but I had to.

"My wife died giving birth to Raiyah. At the proudest moment of my life, I lost her. And it kills me everyday just to look at the girl and wondering how such a thing could happen. I know I shouldn't blame her, but I'm convinced it's her fault."

I didn't know what to say. I had, truly, never seen such a tormented soul. These past years, I envisioned Abbas as a cold, heartless man. But I never really knew him.

He continued, "Things were fine at first. It took me a while to adjust without her. I still feel the pain and I pray that one day she'll appear to me once again. She doesn't even come in my dreams. I have only a few photographs of her. I feel like I'm betraying her by allowing Raiyah to stay with me. I just can't do it

"But she has to stay; if not for me, then for herself. I admit, Raiyah and I . . . we have our differences. She's not exactly my biggest fan," Abbas said with a tired smile.

He turned to look at the window. His reflection looking back at him, he closed his eyes.

"I've been a terrible father, haven't I?"

I finally said, "No, not at—"

Abbas held a hand up. "Please. I know I have. I've been a terrible person, Faraz, but more importantly, I've been a terrible father. I know that. Just listen . . . don't take her from me. I'll be better now, I promise."

The rain had somehow found its way in my eyes. I wiped my cheeks of my tears and said, "If you really love your wife, Abbas uncle, you'll let her leave. She doesn't deserve this. I'm sorry about your wife; truly, I am. But don't you think she would have wanted Raiyah to be happy? More than anything, I think that was your wife's last thought before she passed away."

He looked up at me again.

I continued, "Call her downstairs. I want you to apologize. Pour your heart out as you did to me. Hug her and tell her that you love her."

He muttered, "She doesn't love me. I must be the first father that has a daughter who hates him."

I ignored his pessimism and said, "Go up there and give it a try."

He looked upstairs then back at me. He walked up those stairs, one at a time, each step resulting in more and more hesitation unless he reached the top.

He knocked on the door and walked in. I watched from downstairs quietly; I heard whispering then crying.

They both walked out of the room and walked down. Raiyah slung her arms around my neck and rested her head on my shoulder.

Abbas sighed and said, "She wants to be with you. She doesn't want to stay here . . . whatever makes her happy, like you said. Just promise me you won't treat her like I did. Promise me that you'll love her."

"Forever," I replied.

He looked at Raiyah now and said, "Call when you get a chance."

She nodded, looking down.

I told Raiyah to go to the car, told her that we were finally going home.

Abbas turned to leave but right before he turned the light off, I had something to say.

"You're an honorable man, Abbas uncle. You're a brave soul and I'm honored to be in your presence. God shall ensure you heaven."

He smiled at me. "Your kind words are too much, Faraz. Some other time, please. I would like to be alone."

He hit the switch and darkness fell over the room.

I stood for about a minute more and then walked out of the house and started up the car.

I didn't ask her what was discussed between her and her father in her room. Honestly, I didn't need to know.

As we were cruising down the road and to my place, she said softly, "I understand him now. He's not that bad."

"Most people aren't, Raiyah, once you finally see them."

—

My father welcomed Raiyah with open arms.

He was a caring man, understanding and noble. Surely by now he had heard the stories of the chaos that ensued in the Pasha household and had no objections when I knocked on the door, asking.

His only concern was that he could not have a young, unmarried woman strolling about in his house. He said it was wrong, dishonorable. I knew the point he was trying to make but at that time, I was still young and afraid of marriage and afraid of commitment. I did love her, I really did; but I guess I suffered from cowardice, Fahad, something I hope that never ails you.

My mother, on the other hand, objected at first, saying she would speak to Raiyah's father and sort everything out. That it was all a big misunderstanding. That's the thing about mothers, Fahad. They are steadfast in the belief that every single thing is a "misunderstanding" and can be easily resolved through kind words. I'm sorry that there won't be a mother to teach you that. Don't get me wrong; kind words can be remarkable at the right time. I'm passing on what I've learned in life. The world doesn't work that way, Fahad, unless you want it to. Will, determines everything. Another thing I want you to remember.

My father had guests over more often now. They would retreat into the den and light cigars where conversation of cricket and politics occurs; however, not anymore. I knew that these men were over to plan wedding arrangements and discuss viable options and possible locations. Once these men would leave, each thanking my father too many times, I would confront him; tell him that I hadn't even proposed yet. His answer was for me to hurry it up; he said I couldn't lose a girl like that.

One day, when the night was lukewarm and the atmosphere thin, I heard him talking to my mother about me. I leaned closer to the door and heard him pacing the room, ranting.

" . . . he just doesn't understand that he doesn't have all the time in the world.

I heard my mother sigh and say, "Give him time. That's all he needs. You know that Faraz needs to think things over before he makes a decision."

My father grunted and replied, "A man who plants a garden must water it, Asmara, and you know that."

She sighed and didn't say anything. I slowly walked away from the door, thinking about what my father said. Was I taking too long? Was I stalling? I knew I loved her, yet, something was holding me back. Then, fear raised its ugly head in my mind and provoked me to think that she might loose interest. Raiyah is beautiful; other men knew that. The mere thought of losing her seemed incredulous to me. I couldn't lose her to another man, I wouldn't allow it.

I kept thinking about this until nightfall came and she bustled in through the door, flustered and cold. I smiled at the sight of her; the lights were off in the room downstairs but suddenly the room was alit.

The look on her face startled me. She was usually always smiling, her eyes vivid and her face glowing. This time, she asked me to sit.

"What's wrong?" I asked her, my eyebrows up. Suddenly, I felt my spirits plummet.

"Faraz," she said, placing her hand on mine, "please be calm when I tell you this."

I stood. "What is it? Tell me."

She looked around the room, panic on her face, "Faraz—"

"Get to the point."

"I have to go to America for two years, Faraz."

My world crashed. What I thought was impossible, what I thought would never happen, happened. Honestly, I knew Raiyah's ambition would be an obstacle but I didn't know it would happen so soon and for two years? I couldn't believe it. I just couldn't.

"T . . . two years?"

She then went on explaining how she received an offer from a school in the U.S. to help her achieve her degree in medicine. How it was her life, how she had no choice but to go. She told me she would be back for me.

I sat listening, numb and heartbroken. Her words were a blur; the sight of her was suddenly a mirage. I slowly stood and walked to my room, shutting the door and wondering why.

They say that love hurts, Fahad, and it never hurt me more than at that time. It stung me and laughed in my face. It's not something that these Disney movies play it up to be, no, no. Love is full of happiness, joy, euphoria yet it also provides hardships and obstacles. Something so powerful, something so wonderful and it hurts.

God shows us all the important people in life early on in life. Your father, your mother, brother, sister, aunt, uncle, best friend, cousins, I could go on and on. Yet, he hides the face of that special someone, the special person you will fall in love with and experience pure elation and then deal with heartache.

She moved the day after. I drove her to the airport and told her I loved her. We stood in front of the gate for the longest time, staring into each other's eyes, drowning in our pupils. Her eyes were like an endless abyss of beauty, something I felt like I was falling into and I couldn't help it.

She boarded the plane that day and I did not see her for the longest time. Phone calls came sporadically, describing America as "brash" and "invigorating". She said it was truly the place she dreamt about, but as time went by, the calls decreased. My father would hint at me that I let her go and I ignored his words, wouldn't dare believe them.

During her absence, I felt empty. Like my other half was missing from my soul. In a way it was. Raiyah's little sister, now seventeen, dropped by the house to talk me into staying in the Pasha household, that it would make me more comfortable. I refused, knowing it would tear me apart to be in her house with photos of her all around.

The first year passed. No phone call for months. I was losing it. And then, finally, a call. Sitting on the chair reading, I hastily grabbed for the phone, blurting out, "Raiyah?"

It was a gruff old man's voice. Sounded like the imam of the local mosque. I asked him what happened. He was quiet and then he said, "Abbas Pasha passed away early this morning. Pills were found near his bed. If you could reach his daughter, please let her kn—."

I dropped the receiver and thought of Raiyah far, far away, not being able to be there at the death and funeral of her father, albeit a father who didn't show his compassion, yet a father. I then remembered I had no means of communication with her, that I hadn't heard her voice in months, that I missed her touch and was angry with myself for letting her go. Some of my friends called me selfish; they told me there would be times that she wouldn't be there; I blew them off but somehow I knew it was true. This would be the first funeral I had ever attended, the first of many. I began thinking about how before she left, their relationship had changed. They exchanged jokes and Raiyah had small ideas of moving back into her house again, so she could fully heal the wound between them. It was too late now and she didn't even know.

The imam told me to call her and tell her what happened. Yet, I didn't call. No one did.

—

The weather was harsh, the wind blowing fast, the clouds protecting the sun. There was a small amount of people there; mostly family and close friends. Aisha, Raiyah's sister, cried throughout. My father kept his face down, silent for the duration of the funeral. My mother held nothing back, however; she bawled harder than Aisha. As for myself, I mirrored my father with a solemn expression and soft eyes.

The imam said a few words. How Abbas was a strong man, strong for raising two young girls by his self. He praised Abbas' audacity and courage for allowing his oldest daughter, Raiyah, to venture out into the daring world of America, where dreams are made and hopes are gained. He said he hoped that Abbas will find his way to heaven and avoid the path down to hell, for he showed in old age how good of a man he truly was. He stated that, in Abbas' case, his guilt and remorse led to good, ultimately. It led to Aisha's placement in a private school; it led to the funding for Raiyah's trip. While the imam was talking, I wondered about redemption. I had done some bad things in my life, some things I regret, some things that rest on my mind late at night and they won't let me sleep.

Yet, later on life, it's what I discovered. That all the guilt and sorrow I felt leading up to my adoption of Fahad, ultimately, brought out the good in me. I worked harder, paid more attention to your schoolwork, became more active in your life, and attended your basketball games even when you begged me not to come.

Some people live for themselves. I live for you, Fahad. I live for you.

—

Raiyah's return both revived and crushed my heart.

It's remarkable at what can happen in two years, Fahad. I distinctly remember her telling she would come back for me. Yet, it wasn't just her that came back.

I got the call on a mellow Sunday morning, a lazy day when the sun slowly rose and the streets were eerily calm. I woke up and smelled the smoke coming from my father's room. I remember thinking that those cigarettes would be the end of him. Hair ruffled and eyes squinting, I stretched and threw the sheets off me.

Pakistan had become something of a standard, a place where I would never leave. It was my home, I was born there. So why didn't I feel like I belonged there? That question has plagued me for years but now, as the looming feeling of being trapped in this place overcame me, I had a sudden desire to just flee. It didn't matter whether Raiyah was with me or not; I just had to get away from this society, from the nagging adults, from the pathetic girls, from the boasting men, from the very idea of this Pakistani society. I simply had to get away.

But how could I? I was never the spontaneous type. How could I simply pack my bags and wander aimlessly, with no destination or purpose? I would trek countless miles under the hot Pakistani sun and, perhaps, find myself in Iran and from there, collect some savings, earn some money and take flight from there to America.

These thoughts troubled me at times. I had been thinking this ever since Raiyah's father passed away. The agony and unfairness of it just angered me. Another question was. Was I ashamed of my own society? Was I ashamed of the superficiality of this system, the idea that if a son doesn't grow up to be a doctor, he and his father are banished and considered a "failure" to the other fathers and sons? Or perhaps the fact that all that mattered at that time was reputation. Yes, that must have been it. That's all a man had back then, and God forbid he lose it. My father had a reputation of being one of the top doctors, and yet, his son wants to dabble with words and illustrations? And simply because of that, our family would become ostracized? The idea seemed completely and utterly preposterous to me and it became clear to me now. I had grown up in a society I hated from day one and, now, I realize this. I'm not one of them. I'm not.

Disrupting my thoughts was the telephone. Ringing violently, I picked the phone up.

"Hello?"

"Faraz," a woman's voice said. "I'm coming home today."

My spirits skyrocketed. I literally yelled. "What time?" I asked while experiencing pure euphoria inside, "I can pick you up and we can go to our spot, and catch up, I missed you so—"

"Faraz. Faraz."

Her voice was cold; it didn't contain the joy and happiness mine did. Slowly, I felt that something had changed. Through a couple of words, she already sounded more cultured and dignified, someone with a sense of maturity and understanding that, seemingly, could only be achieved through visiting the great land of America.

She continued, "Faraz . . . I've found someone."

—

The airport was drab, messy; the complete opposite of O'Hare Int'l. I skimmed the crowd for her illuminating green eyes, a pair of pupils that would add some color and light to such a dreary place. True, it had been such a long time, and some of her features escaped my memory, but I would never forget the eyes.

Suddenly, I felt a tap on the shoulder. I turned and was ambushed by her, a broad smile on her face, her white teeth lighting up my face.

"You've gotten taller!" she remarked, as she circled me, as if I was some exhibit at a museum, "But, your hair?" She frowned, "Time for a haircut, Roz—Faraz."

I caught her mistake and stared into her eyes, making sure she knew I heard it. Her smile vanished and she looked away. I then looked past her and spotted a tall, fit man with a scruffy beard in a black suit. He was looking away though; chatting with some other people.

"What's his name?"

"Salman."

I looked down, sighed.

I looked at her again and whispered, "I never wanted anyone else. I only wanted you."

She didn't look at me. She was looking down, looking away. I felt empty; the emptiest kind of anger. This man probably had money, loads of it, a big house, a fancy car. What did I have?

"I'll still come and see you," she started, "I will and we can-"

"No," I interrupted. "Don't. Don't bother. You didn't even have the decency to give me a chance. I was up, night after night, waiting for you to call, waiting for you to let me know where you were; now I see you were too busy walking around with this phony guy."

She didn't say anything again and I went onward, "I missed you so much. You don't even know. Ask anyone back home . . . I'll never find anyone else, you know."

"Things change, Faraz." She was looking at me now. "We were kids. What did we know? I have a job here now, I have a house, and I'm settling down . . . some things just don't last. But I'll never forget you, you know that."

I wasn't listening. How the hell could I hear something like that? I was a man watching a train pull away, a man witnessing the collapse of a building.

"I hope he makes you happy," was all I said and walked away.

He walked over now and held his hand out, "Hey chief, gone so soon?"

I wanted to punch him. But I turned around and grinned; shook his hand.

"Raiyah's told me a lot about you," he laughed with his arm around her. "Good man, good man." He had the voice of a news anchor, loud with a lot of unnecessary laughing. He was the fakest person I had ever seen.

All I did was nod and that put him off guard a bit. He checked his watch and whistled. Raiyah was looking at the floor.

Something beeped; their cue to head toward the gate.

"See you chief," he said. I wished he wouldn't call me that.

"Take care," Raiyah said, smiling. They turned and headed for the gate, his arm around Raiyah Pasha as they headed toward a new life. She looked back and waved and all I could do was wave back.

———

Years passed and the pain eased. At first, I had become the laughing stock of the community, known as the one who let her get away. My father simply looked at me with a disheartened expression upon his face followed by a heavy sigh when I told him the news. He turned and went into his room and I stood in the kitchen, light shining on me, and I had never felt more scrutinized. His intentions were good; he was just disappointed. He wondered about what would happen to me, when I would finally start a life of my own, when I would get a job and become successful. Sometimes, I think all his concern about me left him with no concern for his self. He smoked constantly and started drinking at home now; he would come home late, stumbling, yelling at my mother to make him something. As always, I would turn in my bed and block the noise out.

One day, however, I received an invitation to a college in India, where I would meet with some professors who thoroughly enjoyed the manuscript of my first lengthy written work. Eagerly, I showed my parents the letter; my father was overjoyed. "You see," he told one of his friends as I left the room, "my son has become something. I told you he would."

I packed for the next couple of days, excited to finally leave and venture out into the world, albeit it being the next country over, but anything was a start. Talk began to circulate in the town, that Waqas' son was invited to a prestigious college in India. Confused, I asked my parents how word spread and they took the blame. I never liked attention nor did I ever ask for it. Yet, my father said the only reason he told people was he thought that I deserved all the interest after what I've been through. It was the first time that either of us had addressed Raiyah. My spirits plummeted and he realized he had made a mistake. He began to apologize but I had already made my way out of the door.

A few days later, it was time for me to depart. We arrived at the train station as a family and waited. I would only be gone for a few days yet parents have the tendency to overreact whenever their children leave for anywhere. Once the train arrived, my mother began weeping. Embarrassed, I told her I would be fine and wiped away her tears. She became calm and then walked away. I now looked at my father, a stern and serious expression on his face. It was always business and professional with him. I gestured to shake his hand and he stood there, eying me.

"Come here," he beckoned and pulled me into our first hug since my childhood.

I pulled away and he nodded at me, sniffed. I smiled and turned; boarded the train. Found a seat and began to drift into a deep sleep.

———

"This is remarkable, Mr. Ahmad."

The windows allowed light to shine in and reflect on the dark mahogany walls and floor. I was sitting at a desk in front of a chalkboard which had been scrawled upon countless times. Three aged men stood in front of me, each complete with full, scruffy beards and thick accents. They were all donned in the same clothing; a neat, ironed dress shirt which was tucked into khaki dress pants with shiny black shoes and a black coat to cover their shirt; buttoned, of course.

The shortest one introduced himself as Dr. Sarker. He proclaimed, "You really have written an excellent piece of work here, Mr. Ahmad. The scenery, the descriptions, the comparisons . . . and you are still so young!"

The pudgy one next to him, Dr. Reddy, quipped, "Yes, yes . . . with age will come even more polished writing."

They continued to analyze and go over the novel with me. I explained to them the themes and ideas behind some chapters. They "oohed" and "ahhed" at some of my explanations and glanced at each other sporadically, eyebrows raised. While I discussed this with them, I noticed the third professor; a tall, slender man with a longer beard than any of them who had remained quiet since he greeted me.

Once I finished going over the book, they sat back and beamed at me.

"Mr. Ahmad," Dr. Sarker began, "you have quite the talent. However, we did not invite you here simply to chit chat with you. You realize that those who possess certain talents must have the audacity to share their gift, no? Mr. Ahmad, this college is in touch with a publishing company, who we have already received confirmation from, that will gladly publish your novel."

A sense of accomplishment rushed through my body. What I had aspired to become my entire life, what I dreamt about becoming, had finally manifested itself into a reality, into truth. No longer would I cower in the face of doubt or failure, no longer would I succumb to the pressures and the "you'll never make it."

Bringing me down from cloud nine was the tall professor, who had remained quiet up until this point. "However," he said slowly, "the publication will take some time. The editors in the company will spend hours correcting your . . . grammatical mistakes." His voice reminded me of the icy, harsh weather of winter. I hated winter.

He continued now, stepping in front of Sarker and Reddy, both of which seemed uneasy. "You have written a decent novel; there is no doubt about that. Yet, I wonder what motivated you to write such a powerful and emotional first novel, hm?"

He was now staring into my eyes, as if he were trying to read my mind, and if he was, he saw the heartbreak I had felt, saw the agony that pained me everyday, saw the long, endless nights where Raiyah wouldn't flee from my mind and I would simply sit at my desk and write, write my feelings away.

Shocking me, he asked suggestively, "Is it a woman?"

Dr. Reddy interjected, "Please, Dr. Shah . . ."

I held a hand up and replied, "Yes."

Dr. Shah now leaned back into a chair and looked at the ceiling, sighed.

"Ah, the woman . . . such a mystery. They are the object of many famous works, you know?"

I nodded sternly; it seemed as if he was trying to get something out of me. He lowered his gaze from the ceiling and surveyed me intently, searching my soul. After a moment, he got up instantly and said, "Best of luck in the future, Mr. Ahmad. Deepak and Vishnu, I will see you at lunch."

The other two professors waved and smiled. Once Dr. Shah was out of earshot, Dr. Sarker whispered, "Don't mind him; he's different."

"I didn't," was my reply.

All three of us watched the man as he whistled and walked briskly down the corridor until he made a turn, disappearing into the campus.

—

I stayed in the city for a few more days, exploring the campus and having a taste of college life. I spent the rest of my time gushing over my achievement; I figured I should call my parents and tell them the news, then I realized I would like to see the expression on their faces once I told them.

Two days later, I was informed that I was a published author. I was thrilled, overjoyed. They gave me a copy to keep and told me that I would be hearing from the company shortly. That I should go back now.

I thanked them and made my way through the messy streets and into the hotel, where I packed my things and made my way toward the train station. I approached the train station and noted that I was early. Sat down on a bench and began feeling the book, flipping through the pages, reading my words on official printed paper, it all felt like a dream . . .

"Faraz?"

I froze. My hand was caught in between flipping to the last chapter and a warm feeling washed over me, a feeling of similarity. I had heard that voice before . . . but no, it couldn't be . . .

"Faraz?"

I looked up now and there she was eyes green as grass, skin fair as day.

"R . . . Raiyah? What are you doing here?"

She stood uncomfortably, eying me. Something, again, seemed different. She was impassive and was wearing glasses now, which rested on the tip of her elegant nose. Her arms were crossed across her chest and she carried a backpack, complete with a bottle of water.

"I'm going home actually . . . it's been too long, Faraz."

She began telling me about Paris then; she didn't mention Ali, but at that time I thought it would be because she didn't want to pain me even more. As she spoke, I kept thinking about how much I missed her; her smell, her touch, her laugh, and her eyes. God, if I could just have that back, I wouldn't care if this book didn't become published or if my father finally seemed proud of me.

Then I remembered how my heart broke. How she broke it, ruthlessly and with no remorse. My eyebrows inadvertently furrowed yet she didn't notice; she was still rambling on about Paris. She had told me she had loved me the day she left. It made me think about the accuracy of that statement. Did she mean it? Did she lie? Was she already getting tired of me by then? Had I become a cancer, a roadblock in her life? Even if it was a lie, it was what I wanted to hear, Fahad. Which made me think, why bother telling the truth if what everyone in the world wants to hear are lies?

I nodded a couple times, looking away, resisting the urge to look into her eyes. But I couldn't help it. As I looked at her, the butterflies in my stomach erupted into life. Did you know I've missed you, I thought, oh God, I've missed you. The train arrived now, coming to a screeching halt. It was by then that she noticed the book in my hand.

She knew what it was at the start. For once, she smiled. "You finally did it, huh?"

"What?"

She pointed her long index finger to the leather-bound novel in my hands and grinned, pushing hair out of her face.

I cracked a smile and nodded. "Yeah . . . I did; that's why I was here."

She replied, "I always knew you would make it."

Silence ensued and I boarded the train. She followed me and as I got on the train, the words slipped out of my mouth.

"Where's Sally?" I said jokingly. My dislike of him had not vanished. But I regretted it as soon as it escaped my mouth.

Her expression grew solemn. Her complexion lightened a little and she clutched her purse just a little bit tighter. Her beautiful emerald eyes began to water and by then, I knew what she was going to tell me.

But I was sick of it, Fahad. I was sick of heartbreak, I was sick of dealing with pain, I was sick of attending funerals and getting unwanted phone calls, I was sick of misery. God, I've been through a lot; haven't I? And yet . . . it just doesn't stop.

She pulled me close now and rested her head on my shoulder. The train had started moving and we were in the back, where no one could see us, where no one could see her weeping.

"Salman is no longer a part of this world, Faraz."

There it was. What I had hoped would never happen, what I hoped would never even come close to happening, did. I knew she was going to tell me . . . but it's different once you hear it said out loud. Her world was crashing, I knew, I could relate. I didn't ask how or why, yet she kept going.

"He was coming home from work one day . . . a day like any other. S . . . some kids thought it would be funny t . . . to cross a red light."

I was quiet, still holding her, her words going directly into my ear.

She continued, "I'm going home now . . . I need some time alone. I would appreciate if you didn't come see me for a few weeks, Faraz. I need to see my father."

My heart broke even more, as if it had been shattered into pieces and left on the ground.

"Raiyah . . . he passed away, before you came back. I wanted to tell you but—"

She slapped me. I felt the sting on my cheek, the heat of her hand against my skin. Her eyes were furious . . . then began to soften. She started crying now.

She turned to leave and right before she went into the opposite section of the train, she said, "I'm sorry that I ruined everything Faraz . . . and I'm sorry that sorry is never enough."

She left and I was alone. I sat down in a seat, staring out the window, rubbing my own cheek, attempting to soothe the pain.

Someone came out to serve drinks.

"Sir, would you like anything?"

I looked at her and waited a moment.

"Yes, please . . . a coffee, with cream and two and half teaspoons of sugar."

While she handed me it, I asked her if she knew why.

"Why, sir?"

"Because she loves it."

—

She went her way; I went mine. Our eyes met at the station back in Pakistan but she began walking the other way. I stood for a while, watching her walk away from me. Sorrow filled my soul.

However, once I got home, all that changed.

It happened exactly how I imagined it would be. I knocked on the door sharply, book in hand. My father opened the door, eyes full of expectation.

"How was the trip? What happened?"

I walked in silently and faced him; showed him the book in my hand.

World's End by Faraz Ahmad.

His eyes welled up with joy and pride and he started flipping through the pages not believing it. He put the book down and demanded a celebration.

I had never seen such happiness simply radiate from my father when I told him the news. He was laughing, smiling . . . God, I missed it. I still do.

He would talk about how he would throw a party. Just for me. When I protested against it; he would shake his head and wag his finger.

"Stop with that bullshit. You've become something; a published author, mashallah. Now, quit whining and start inviting."

That was the thing about my father. He had a certain brashness about him; he wasn't shy or ashamed to voice his opinions. He told me my modesty was certainly an admirable trait of mine but that sometimes I shouldn't be so unsure.

He called half the town; maybe even more. The news spread like wildfire. Kamal congratulated me and said I was the main topic of the people in the bazaars. I wondered how it would be after this; I found myself staying up thinking about where I would go from there? Stay with the family or discover my dreams in America?

The party was on a Friday; the moon was amazingly bright that night and the stars were dazzling.

I showed up to the applause of countless strangers; faces I had never seen before and some only a few times here and there when my mother would entertain or when my father would have his smoking sessions. They all shook my hand and smiled at me; I must have shook a hundred hands that day; maybe more.

When it was dinner time, as I was eating with Kamal, I noticed Raiyah out of the corner of my eye. She was walking alone to the balcony outside; she had always been fascinated with the stars. I never knew exactly why. I figured that they must give her hope, these stars that are consistent in their brilliance and provide light and guidance for those who are lost.

She was lost at that time. She didn't know what to do with herself. She had lost her vigor, her passion ever since Ali passed.

I told Kamal that I was going to talk to Raiyah and he pulled me down.

"Faraz . . . it's over. She's heartbroken right now . . . what can you do?"

I stared at him, "It's never over . . . not with her. It's different with her, Kamal."

He sighed heavily and said, "Do as you wish. Keep an eye out for the gossiping aunties."

I nodded and walked through the crowd, leaving the music filled atmosphere and entering the balcony where she had both arms resting on the ledge, staring out into the horizon. It was a cold night and she was shivering. Without saying anything, I took my coat off and put it on her.

She turned, startled. Then she saw me and was calm.

"Oh, Faraz."

I gave away a small smile and asked, "How are you?"

She sighed, "Could be better; you?"

"Same; what are you doing out here?"

She turned back and looked up now at the moon. "Missing you."

I turned away and said, "Raiyah . . ."

She turned around and said, "I can't stop thinking about you. I do it all the time now, I miss your smell, your touch, your jokes . . . I love all of it. I love you."

"It's not fair of you to say that," I said as she draped her arms around me, "it's not fair."

She looked into my eyes and I looked away. For some reason, I was angry with her. God, I couldn't contain my emotion anymore. Sometimes I was in pure, unadulterated love with her and sometimes I hated her.

"You know, our parents were always right. It's good to be home. It always is."

I looked out into the city and said, a bit harshly, "Well, whoever told you to go to Paris?"

She was quiet and I realized my mistake. She took a step forward and stared at the city beneath our gaze. She pointed to a small part of town, illuminated by the flickering street lights.

"I can't believe I grew up there. In that little part of town, a piece of the pie that is Pakistan . . . I miss it, you know. I miss being young and careless and be—"

She paused then continued, "Being with you."

I couldn't believe what I was hearing. She had fell in love with a man from America who just passed away and now she was telling me she wanted to be with me again. I didn't want her to do me any favors or for her to feel obliged that she had to be with me, because there was no other way now.

And then, "Faraz . . . I don't think we can be together now. I mean, we're older now, we're headed down different roads, different paths, we want different things from life, Faraz, please understand—"

"I love you," I said as I looked into her eyes, refusing to let them calm me down. "I love you; that's all that should matter. Damn it Raiyah, you can't do this to me. Who gives a damn where you're going or if you want to leave here and never look back? And how would that affect you and me, how would that affect us?"

She took a step forward toward me and her eyes welled up, "You, you want to write books for a living, Faraz! I want to make something out of my life! If that means, going back and leaving this hell and you, that's what I'll have to do. You always told me to follow my dreams, did you mean it?"

I almost said something back when there was a tap on the glass door behind us. We both turned around, our faces flushed from the anger; it was visibly showing on our facial expressions. My father stood at the door, one eyebrow raised.

"Everything okay?" he asked.

Raiyah was weeping now and it killed me to look at her and say everything was fine. It killed me, Fahad.

I walked out and left both of them staring at each other. I walked outside and it was raining now. I wandered aimlessly for about five minutes. I needed a drink, yes, that's it.

I saw some old friends sitting on the block with several bottles and I walked on over. I sat down and they all roared with approval.

"I have a story," I said as the rain pelted me.

"Take a bottle first," the man to the right of me said.

I took a sip and began spilling my heart out.

—

It was raining hard now and I was stumbling. Holding the arm of the man next to me for support, I said, "Look, I'm not a good man. I'm not. And to her, to her, I'm just a joke."

The men murmured in disapproval and tried to get me to sit down, but I continued, "But the first time, the first time I did something for a girl, I messed up. Is that a mistake?"

"No, Bhai, drop it, come on."

I pushed him away violently, the rain falling harder now. I stood now, staring at the sky. Then down at my feet.

I said softly, "Yes it is such a mistake . . . that I made her cry. Tell me, why, when her tears, when they fall from her eyes, why does it hurt here?"

I pointed to my heart now, my hot tears mixing with the cold rainwater; the gray and gloomy skies lingered above.

"Understand?" I asked.

"Yes, Bhai, I do . . ."

I snorted. "What do you understand? She says I don't understand anything . . . but then how do I understand the love between us?"

I sat now, tired and weary. "I swear; I don't know what to do anymore. If she was here . . . I would be speechless."

"She's behind you."

I waved him off.

"No, really!"

I sighed heavily and turned to see her there, a black umbrella shielding her from those wretched raindrops. I remember thinking how she could avoid the physical raindrops but never the ones of sorrow that fell on her throughout her life and I shut my eyes.

I turned back around. "Put the drinks down," I muttered. "It's not polite to drink in front of a lady."

Then I got up with my bottle and proclaimed, "But I can drink because I'm not polite, Raiyah . . . I'm not a nice guy . . ."

Raiyah stepped forward and gently placed her hand on my arm. My eyes closed at her touch; it had been too long.

"Let's go home now, Faraz."

I stammered, "I . . . I'm not a good m . . . man, Raiyah . . . I'm not . . ."

Then I made eye contact as we made our way through the rain, under a single black umbrella, paving our path back home to what life used to be for us and what we hoped and prayed for it be.

I looked at her through the raindrops and saw a beacon of hope in my life, Fahad. My parents, God bless them, never reached Raiyah's level. She was my inspiration, my encouragement, my second soul. That's what love is, I think; a soul's recognition of its counterpart. My father always told me I wasn't in love, that I was too young to understand something so complex. He gave me a bit of advice: if I ever had one doubt about Raiyah, then it wasn't love. I never had that doubt, Fahad, never. You see, amidst all the arguments and hardship both she and I went through, we made it. Sure, I may have gotten angry at her, scolded her, even ignored her, but I never left her side. Even then, when I stormed out of the hotel where the party was at, rage and anger had consumed me. My judgment was blinded. And for that, I apologized to her every day.

You're far too young to understand all this now, but bear with me . . . . Someday you will find your own Raiyah.

—

You looked up at me, captivated by my story, eyes wide. Night had fallen; the streetlights outside shone and emitted some light into our house through the windows.

I continued, "We got married shortly after. Maybe a couple of months later. We moved here, to Chicago. And then . . . she died. And my world was black, Fahad. All I have is you."

You were looking down now. I got up slowly and turned to walk to my bedroom when I heard you whisper an apology.

Glancing back at you, I said, "You don't need to apologize. Nothing is your fault."

You looked up again and nodded. Came over and hugged me.

"You loved her a lot, didn't you?"

"Yes," I answered. "Yes, I did . . . I still do, Fahad, I still do."

CHICAGO, 2001

"Yes, Mr. Holloway, I understand."

There was a fan whirring above me again as I received more bad news. The lights were dim and Mr. Holloway, the principal, sat behind the desk with his arms crossed and a tired look on his face. He let out an exasperated sigh and shrugged his shoulders; it seemed as if he didn't know what to do with you anymore.

He leaned forward now, his elbows resting on the mahogany desk. "We've tried everything with Fahad. It just seems he's not that interested in . . . school, frankly."

I looked away now, out the window and remembered the days of my childhood where I wasn't that interested in school and I would come home with a droopy face and my father would know instantly. I heard the method of punishment here was grounding. Back in Pakistan, grounding was unheard of; it seemed like a weak, mediocre method. He would yell and shout and sometimes when I came home bearing a note that stated I was doing horribly, he would have no restraint on his right hand toward my cheek.

But here, in the great land of America, that wasn't possible. I loved my father but I promised myself I would never stoop to that level. Unfortunately, anger is a strong emotion and it gets the best of us sometimes. I would let slip some harsh words and maybe raise my hand a couple of times and I felt by doing that, I betrayed myself.

The principal concluded, "Fahad is a nice kid, but I just think he needs some extra motivation."

Shaking his hand and letting him know I'd do my best as I left the school just didn't seem like it would fix anything. As much I didn't like to admit it, he was right. You were different from me, did you know that? In every way, I was shy, timid, and hesitant; you were outgoing, rebellious, eager.

As I entered the parking lot into the cool night air of Chicago and opened the car doors and began to make my way back home, I thought that being too lenient on you in your childhood was a mistake. Sure, I would hear that you often got in arguments at school but I thought nothing of it; how could a first grader cause any real trouble?

Now you were thirteen, you were growing up and discovering what goes in the world. You understood the difference between right and wrong, good and bad and yet . . . I had an uneasy feeling sometimes. You see, the world is a dangerous place. It's full of secrets and deception and betrayal. When you got in arguments with me about why you couldn't go out on that Saturday night or why you couldn't carpool with your friend who's a senior at the high school, that's when I missed Raiyah the most. I missed her logic, I missed her ability to convince; I was sure she could turn you in the right direction. I felt like you were going down a dark tunnel at that point and the only thing that felt worse was that I couldn't do anything about it.

I entered the house to silence except the stereo blasting in your room upstairs. As soon as I entered the music stopped and I heard a thud. Then you keep bustling down the stairs, wiping your long hair out of your face and smirking.

"What'd he say?"

I sighed and pointed to a seat on the couch. With a sigh, you knew what was coming. You sat down with a plop, disgruntled already. Staring at me with those green eyes, you asked, "Well?"

I rubbed my eyes and looked at you. "I spoke to your principal. He said you need motivation . . ."

You replied, "I don't need anything. School's just hard right now but it'll get better."

You started to fiddle your thumbs and stared at the floor.

I let out an exasperated sigh and said, "Look, Fahad, you can't goof off that much anymore. You're in high school now; you need to act like it."

I paused then continued, "You're grounded. No TV, no video games, no hanging out with that Andre kid anymore, he's nothing but trouble . . . ."

You stood now and, your voice a little higher, "Oh? So who should I hang out with then? That lady who you like so much down the street, her son? Is that it? "Cause he brings great grades and is in honors so the fact that he's an arrogant as . . . ."

"Go to your room," I said.

You started to say something else but I repeated myself.

Turning around and marching up the stairs, you slammed the door shut. I stood with a look of surrender on my face and sat on the couch again.

I remembered Raiyah then . . . a long time ago . . .

—

The moon was shining bright above us as we lay in the grass, just looking at the stars. We were sixteen or seventeen, not a care in the world. She nudged me and asked me, "Do you believe in love?"

I looked back into her eyes and whispered, "Ever since I met you."

She blushed and turned the other way; I grabbed her arm and pulled her back. "Why?"

She sighed and said, "I don't know, I've been thinking about it a lot lately, like what love really is, you know? I find it such a shame that love only seems real in books and movies but never in real life. Why does the greatest thing in the world only belong in fiction, Rozzy? It's troubling me. And another thing . . . ."

"I love you . . . did you know that?"

She was quiet and then lit up my world by smiling. We both stood and she hugged me tight and we rocked side to side.

I leaned in until I was sure I could whisper in her ear and gently said, "God bless the guy who gets you."

"Oh, Faraz . . ."

—

"So who wants to tell me what Lincoln's achievements were?"

The birds chirped outside the classroom's window and the sun shone bright.

The teacher, Ms. Allen, frowned a little once no one raised their hands. She walked around and noticed you, the hood of your jacket covering your face, fast asleep.

"Mr. Ahmad, would you care to join us?"

You woke up slowly and looked around. You said that someone had told you the question and you were about to answer when it happened.

At first some thought it was just a movie—or maybe just a small mishap with the pilot. That's how ridiculous it looked. But it wasn't.

There was a knock on the door and it was another teacher. She held a folder up so the students couldn't see what she saying and whispered something to Ms. Allen.

You said your teacher began to back up slowly and hit the desk. She then ordered you and your peers, in a tone you said you never heard before, into a line and head straight for the cafeteria.

There, your principal informed the students that two planes had struck the Twin Towers in New York City.

———

You came home that day distraught and thinking furiously. You walked in without saying a word and sat on the couch, eyes glued on the coverage of the attacks by CNN. Al-Qaeda's name flashed all over the screen. I couldn't believe what was happening either. This would change things, I remember thinking. I worried about you, about what would happen at school, would you get bullied? American flags were in high abundance from then on, in every place you can imagine. Headlines read "Today we are all Americans" and Bush did not hesitate; he boldly promised that those responsible will be punished. In bookstores, in coffee shops, in supermarkets, in movie theaters; the words Afghanistan and Pakistan was all I heard. I went to Kroger a few days after and as I walked by, I heard a man tell his wife, "All these Moslems will be the end of us." It pained me to hear that, but I was never the type to confront him. It's up to God, I always believed, to punish the ignorant. However, you would have took off running and get in the man's face. You're a brave soul and sometimes I wonder about how different we are and if you realized it too, which you eventually did.

You spoke softly then, "They're Muslims too, right?"

I sighed and sat closer to you. "They don't belong to any religion, Fahad. They're heartless and they know nothing but evil. Don't think that you're associated with these . . . these demons."

"But we are," you said a little louder. "They call themselves Muslims and so do we."

I was quiet and then you gulped and said some kids asked you if your family was behind the attacks.

We sat there for a while, just quiet, just the two of us and you hugged me tight and let it all out. I rubbed the back of your head, telling you it would be ok, just like all parents tell their kids when they knew it wouldn't be ok. It wouldn't be ok when these jokes continue and it wouldn't be ok when you have to deal with them.

Times were getting difficult back then. I knew that you were being thrust into the real world at an early age, realizing you didn't have a complete family and that you never will and seeing other kids that drop out of school because their parents don't care. When I took on the responsibility of raising you, I knew it wouldn't be easy. But it was Raiyah's wish, her desire. I had to honor that, if I didn't honor anything else.

As we watched the fiery towers on TV, you in my arms, I realized that you had fallen asleep. I gave away a slight grin and gently moved out of the way.

As I walked away, I saw you lying on the couch in perfect peace. I read somewhere that dreams are always better than reality and I had a feeling you couldn't wait to go to sleep.

—

It was a cold night in November and a bunch of school friends, with you amongst them, were crowded around a table. The candlelight flickered and shone on Faizan Amin for his sixteenth birthday. You argued and complained about going, but ultimately, you had to.

He blew the candles out and everybody clapped; Ridah walked over and told everyone to take a picture. Cameras flashed, white lights blinded some and then everybody sat around and enjoyed the cake. While you ran off with your friends and Faizan, Ridah approached me and asked if I could talk.

I nodded and followed her into the den where she sat on the couch and put her face in her hands.

"What's the matter?"

She looked up and brushed the hair out of her face—looked out of the window.

"Amin called. Told me he would be stopping by in the next week or sometime close to that. I . . . I don't know where he is or why he's even bothering . . ."

I was listening closely now and asked, "Did he say anything else?"

She threw her hands up in the air and they fell to her side; she seemed exhausted. "Just that he was sorry and that he's a changed man now . . . but I don't want to tell Faizan. He gets so emotional about his father, Faraz. He told me he never wants to see him again but now . . ."

"You should tell him," I said. "Let him know ahead of time so he can take it in and not be surprised when he shows up randomly."

She said she guessed that was true and that it might turn out to be really bad. I gave her a friendly hug and told her that if she ever needed anything, I was right down the street. She nodded and you were standing at the stairs, ready to leave. We said goodbye to everyone and headed out; we were going to walk home.

You had forgotten your coat so I said I would go get it; you said it was resting on the back of one of the chairs in the kitchen table. As I made my way back into the house, the rest of boys were upstairs and it was just Faizan and Ridah in the kitchen with Faizan cleaning some dishes.

I heard Ridah say, " . . . might stay for a little while."

Faizan was quiet; the silence was unnerving.

"He's your father—," she pleaded but he interrupted.

"He left us, Mom . . . . sending us a check every two months doesn't make him a father and it never will."

He stopped cleaning and put both arms on the sides of the sink.

He continued after a bout of more silence, "Tell him not to bother . . . he'd be wasting his time coming back just like he's wasted mine."

He suddenly made his way toward me. Startled, I abruptly knocked lightly on a surface of some table and said, "I think Fahad left his coat in here?"

Ridah sniffled and nodded. Handed me the coat and gave me a knowing look.

I turned and saw Faizan staring intently at something upstairs. I waited till he moved and then I saw it. It was a picture of him at birth and his father, both smiling, smiling as if the world had no problems, and men didn't walk away and wives didn't pass away. Smiling as if everything will be alright and there would be no arguments, no quarrels. They believed in a perfect world, Fahad, and that's something that both of us never did.

I walked outside and you were waiting there with your arms crossed, staring out into the depths of the neighborhood.

"What are you thinking about?"

You turned and said, "I was just thinking how temporary life can be . . . nothing lasts, Dad."

"Some things last," I said and we walked down the street together toward another incomplete household, where we would grow and argue and cry and laugh. We would bicker and fight and it broke my heart but, I never told you this, I couldn't ask for a better son.

———

A few days passed and Ridah sat outside her house in the rocking chair, anxious yet nervous, excited yet betrayed. The sun went up and down every day and Amin didn't show. She would give up with a sigh and enter the house again, and Faizan would grin and tell her that she's wasting her time.

"I told you so," he would say angrily, "he won't come back."

Throughout my life, I was told miracles don't exist; that they simply existed in movies and books and would never be manifested in real life. My father would light countless cigars as he spoke about this to me, or what he liked to call "trimming the fat." He said those who believed in miracles were "wishful thinkers" and that they should be happy with what life has given them. He strongly disliked complainers, for he believed there was always someone worse off than the one complaining. So, I grew up with no dreams of everything every other child dreamt of. I didn't believe that rain would magically fall from the sky after months and months of a drought or that one day all the countries in the world would one day resolve their differences; back then, all these things were considered miracles.

However, when my doorbell rang one Sunday evening and I went to go get it, I believed.

A physical specimen of a man with a semi-lengthy beard and dark brown eyes dressed in polo and jeans stood there. He was looking at his feet and had a suitcase lying face down next to him. His fingers were calloused; his eyes looked tired. They really are the window to the soul. Tired of not being there, I supposed.

He looked up slowly and at the sight of me, I felt his spirits drop. He asked, "Excuse me . . . is Ridah home?"

I gulped and replied, "She lives three houses down from here."

He sighed and said, "My name is Amin . . . I . . . ."

"I know who you are," I interrupted. "I know Ridah as well."

Silence hung between us before he said, "I, uh, I'm her husband. I came here to . . . ."

"I can take you there," I replied, putting on my overcoat.

He looked at me straight now and said that he'd like that.

You were at your friend's house so at that point I figured I would help resolve this situation and then pick you up.

We proceeded to walk toward her house and Amin began to tremble.

"How much has she told you?" he asked, still looking down.

"Enough," was my reply and we approached the door.

I looked at him expectedly and gestured toward the door. He sighed and knocked on the door.

Footsteps were moving around in the house and there was some bustling. More steps. Then, the door opened up.

Amin smiled a little and there, in the doorway, stood Ridah.

She took a step back and crossed her arms. Stared at him for about a minute, taking the sight in, for she didn't know how long he would be here or if she would ever see him again. He then held his arms out and both shared a warm embrace.

"Would you like some tea?" she asked, albeit semi-harshly.

"Yes," he replied and we walked in.

——

The teacup trembled in his hand and he took sporadic sips. He looked around the house in awe and pride.

"You have a beautiful house," he complimented Ridah.

Ridah wasn't flattered. "Thanks," she said calmly.

Silence ensued. He coughed awkwardly and she asked, "Why?"

"Why, what?"

"Why did you come back?" she asked. "Do you know how much you've hurt Faizan? Once he sees you in his house . . . lord knows what he'll do?"

Amin stood and put his hands up, "If he could just let me explain . . . ."

"You don't know him," Ridah said, pointing her index finger at him. "You never will."

Amin was about to say something when there was a slam of the front door.

"I'm home," Faizan announced. "I'm starvi . . . ."

He saw Amin standing there and pointed his finger at him.

"What's he doing here? I didn't know cowards showed their faces."

Amin took a step forward and tried to put his hand on Faizan's shoulder when he spat, "Stay away from me." He turned to his mother now and said, "How could you let him inside our house?"

Ridah was quiet and seemed to be on the verge of tears. I began to make my way out of the house; this was going downhill fast. As I exited the house, Faizan bumped past me and walked out.

Amin called after him, "Faizan, don't walk away."

Faizan called back, "You taught me how."

——

Faizan didn't come home for a while that day. The sun fell and the moon rose and there was no tapping on the door, no signal of entrance. Amin sat on the stairs, saying it was a mistake to come back, but Ridah assured him it would be okay. That tends to happen in life as I've mentioned before, Fahad, when people always say it will be okay when they are sure it won't. It seems to be the universal thing to say when the present looks grim or when the future doesn't seem too bright. The light at the end of the tunnel isn't always bright no matter how much we want it to be. You see, life . . . life is something miraculous. It is filled with love, with joy, hate, friendship, betrayal; countless emotions swerving in and out every day. You heard the optimists say that "everything will be fine in the end" but I've never heard anything more ridiculous.

Don't get me wrong, I've had my faith and my beliefs but they have diminished over the years as I've transformed into a full adult and realized the countless responsibilities, the pressures of everyday life and the burden of being a minority and a Muslim in a post 9/11 America. Ever since Raiyah passed, it's like someone took my hope and smashed it with a hammer; I no longer look at things with undying confidence but instead what is expected and what is real. It is real that Faizan couldn't forgive Amin for a while and it is real that it takes a lifetime to build a trust yet only a second to lose it. People over the years have complained that such things are unfair; however, life is unfair, Fahad. You can't always get what you want. You can't like a girl and immediately expect her to want you back and both of you live happily ever after. She may not even have any feelings for you. You can't wish for your best friend and you to start speaking again, even though you haven't spoken in so long . . . its a matter of life, Fahad, these things can't be changed. Robert Frost once said with great simplicity, life goes on. Life goes on.

Life went on for Faizan as he approached our house and rang the doorbell. You opened the door and his eyes were red; he had been weeping for a while.

Looking down, he muttered, "Fahad . . . I know we haven't been the best of friends but could I please crash here tonight?"

I was about to come downstairs to let Faizan in then I decided to see what you would do. Would you portray my qualities and live through me, allowing Faizan to sleep here tonight or would you shut the door in his face and send him back to an ungrateful father and a broken-hearted mother?

In the end, you let him in. You patted him on the back and got him a couple comforters. As you showed him the guest room, I felt a surge of pride throughout me. Maybe there was hope, I thought after I headed to my room for the night . . . maybe there was hope.

—

The most important lesson in life is how to learn to forgive and forget. From the streets of China and the overwhelming Great Wall to the beaches of California, people make mistakes and argue but in the end they forgive. Somewhere two friends forgive each other and promise that no girl is ever worth a friendship, somewhere a couple forgives each other because their love won't allow them to argue for long. The idea of reconciling and making peace is something remarkable about this world, Fahad; a world where some people hold grudges till the very end and some can't find it themselves to be angry for a day.

Faizan, I suppose, was stuck in between—enraged at his father yet in shock that he actually exists, that he actually came back. His mother has learned to forgive, why hasn't he? Faizan would argue that he had a right to be angry, that he was robbed of a father; thus, he was robbed of a complete childhood. That's the thing about broken families, Fahad . . . they never seem right like an orchestra without a cellist or a nation without a leader. There was no Amin at basketball games, no Amin at birthday parties, no Amin at honors banquets. Faizan never saw his father for sixteen years but the name, the distant face, all remained in the back of his mind. It pained him how out of place Ridah looked at the games, cheering alongside countless fathers who came to the games to watch their sons play and then go to get a bite after the game. Faizan never got his bite to eat; he always went straight home.

He approached me once he came home from school.

"I'm not sure what to do . . . I don't want to forgive him . . ."

"Before you consider that," I sighed. "You need to forgive yourself."

—

He returned to his home late that night, standing outside the doorway in the chilly night air. His mother was asleep and heard yells from the basketball court down the street.

He knocked twice and patiently waited. The door creaked open, and there was his father; his eyes were red.

"Faizan . . ."

The boy burst into tears and jumped into his father's arms, a place so unfamiliar yet friendly, foreign yet welcoming.

"I'm sorry," they both sputtered through their tears over and over again.

Later on, I would see them playing basketball or driving around, sometimes just sitting on the porch talking. They were always laughing, it seemed. They had recovered their perfect world.

As far as I know, Amin never explained his absence and Faizan never asked . . . I guess some stories aren't meant to be told.

———

A year passed, and life had resumed its normalcy. I had a set schedule for every week, and I was set to release my next novel. You would be resuming your sophomore year of high school after this winter break. Ridah, Amin, and Faizan all lived happily now; there were no quarrels or arguments, simply happiness. Everything was perfect.

I would work throughout the week, meet with agents, go to signings, and talk to local high schools. On Fridays, I would go and watch a movie or perhaps meet up with fellow Chicagoan writers and discuss strategies and styles of writing. I spent my Saturdays with you mainly; we would either go watch the Bulls play or rent a movie and relax at the house. What I noticed though is that you seemed less reluctant to spend time with me now. I would ask what your plans were this Saturday, and you would slowly say you already had plans with friends. There was no apology, no sorrow. It seemed as if we were drifting apart, as if you realized we weren't as similar as every other parent and their kid; physically, personally, mentally . . . we were different. I would read a book; you would go and play basketball for hours on end. I would go for a run; you would sit at home and have movie marathons. It irked me to see how carefree you seemed, how relaxed. I only wish I could lose all my stress like you did . . . but I never did.

On Sundays I would visit the cemetery, where the wind always blew gently and the leaves bustled about the graveyard. I would have two bouquets of flowers with me always time; an assortment of tulips, roses, and daisies. I would stop at my father's grave first, the father who came to America in his time of need, of desperation, hoping this great country would cure him. I would only linger around for a minute or two and then place the flowers beside his tombstone and pray for God to forgive his sins.

Then I approached Raiyah's grave. With every step, my memory of her grew stronger, more complete, like a puzzle. With each step, her nose appeared then her mouth, her two eyes, and then her hair, and so on and so forth. Sometimes I would weep, but now I know she wouldn't want me to. She would want me to go on living my life and follow the same advice

I told her about Ali. She was different from the other women, Fahad. Most people didn't understand, and I can only hope that one day those people discover true love in all its glory and what that love really means, a love like a calm river, yet as fierce as a hurricane. Raiyah and I shared a quiet but deep love, something that I was truly blessed with. I would place the bouquet on the ground and sit next to it.

"I miss you so much," I said out loud, looking at her grave. "Fahad's so old now . . . I wish you were here to see him, to teach him about life . . . you were good at that, you know."

I stared at the myriad of graves and just thought about all these people, their families, their loved ones. Most of these people, I figured, never did anything wrong. They probably didn't steal or lie or cheat . . . yet the good seem to die young. Why is that? Why is it that the righteous, the noble, become part of the earth itself while the rich and arrogant live on? I realize now that fairness doesn't play a part in life or death . . . death comes to everybody, it's simply a matter of time. I admit, I'm scared, but not because I would lose my life; but, because I would be leaving behind a child, who's struggling to find his way in a complex world and Kamal—Kamal who's always been there for me. I would spend at least twenty minutes just sitting there, thinking.

I returned home that afternoon to a voicemail on the home phone. Throwing my keys on the counter, I hit play.

" . . . Faraz? This is Kamal, Bhai. I am coming to America next week with the family, I was hoping we all could spend some time, I would love to meet your son."

Kamal? In America? Before I had a chance to digest the information, you walked in the kitchen bearing a jersey and basketball shorts. Twirling a basketball, you asked, "Who was that?"

"A friend from Pakistan" I said, as you cringed at the country's name, "Is coming to visit soon. Fahad, I need you to be on your best behavior."

"Yeah," you replied absentmindedly, already not listening but instead scavenging through the cabinet for some snacks.

"Fahad, did you hear me?"

"Yeah, I got you, best behavior . . . relax," you assured me with a full mouth as your walked back outside.

You turned the corner and disappeared. I turned around and began to make tea.

"Relax . . ." I repeated as I placed the cup in the microwave, "Relax . . ."

—

The past is a strange thing. My father warned me to never dwell on the past; he would sit me on his lap and wag his finger at me, cautioning me to be careful. He would then sit back and light another one of his infamous cigars; say that it was always best to forget.

Truthfully, I had no plans to see Kamal after I departed from Pakistan. Ever since we were children, all Kamal told me was that I had a future, that I would grow up and leave for the great land of America, and he would just stay behind and take care of what his father started. Kamal was never one to venture out into foreign places yet somewhere he was in a plane flying over the Atlantic on his way here with a wife and a kid, a kid who would have nothing in common with you.

You enjoyed sports and movies and you weren't the biggest fan of school. Kamal would boast to me how Ali was a top student at the school in Pakistan and ask how many honors classes you were taking, which college you would like to attend. When I mentioned these things to you, you would wave me off and say that school there was probably "a joke".

You had begun to loath anything even remotely resembling your culture, your heritage. You never accompanied me to the small Pakistani gatherings around the city anymore, where the aunties gossiped and the uncles smoked. You refused to partake in anything cultural at your school, even when you were offered a spot in the school's play on diversity. You declined without thinking, without a second guess. You would avoid the other desi kids at school at all costs, as if association with them might hurt your reputation, your stature in the high school. You would no longer receive invites to parties every weekend or be handed the ball and the opportunity to hit the game-winning shot in basketball games anymore. Not if you hung out with the Patels' and the Saleems'. No way, you responded when I told you that Aamir Patel's mom called and asked if you would like to come over to Aamir's house one day.

"Are you kidding me?" you asked with a eyebrow raised, thumb on phone, texting away.

"Well, she did invite you . . ."

You turned your attention back to your phone. "I'm hanging with Andre and the boys this weekend. Tell her I'm sick or something."

It would go on like that for a while. You went out whenever you could and didn't really have much interest in staying home.

But there was one night I never forgot. It was a cold night; the leaves flew around the sidewalks of Chicago. It was the championship game of your sophomore season. You made me promise I would come so I cancelled a signing and headed over to the high school.

Soon enough, I was sitting in the bleachers, scanning the court for #3. It took me a minute, but I noticed you as you were warming up, launching three pointers and looking around the court. We made eye contact and I winked. You grinned and turned around. Swish; the game went down to the wire. You were down by four points with twenty-seven seconds left in the game. Your team inbounded it in and your friend Andre Carter ran up the court, eying his defender and looking for an open player. He faked a shot and then found you cutting baseline and you made a lay-up. The whistle was blown, and you would be going to the line for one more.

The crowd was raucous now; signs sprung up throughout the crowd, some had your name on it, your number. None of it mattered to you as you dribbled twice and effortlessly nailed the shot.

The other team called a timeout and as you walked back to the bench you looked at me with a knowing look. Then I knew. Before it even happened I knew.

The game resumed and the other team rushed it up the court and made a bad pass. It was intercepted by you and you sprinted up the court. Twelve seconds. Two on one. You passed to Andre. Nine seconds. Andre went up to the three-point line and passed it back. Four seconds. Staring at the clock, you dribbled once and pulled up in your opponents face, just inside the arc. One second.

I never heard a crowd get so quiet in one second. While the ball was in the air, all that was heard was the buzzer sounding. However, once the shot went in smoothly and the scoreboard showed the change in the score by a mere two points signaling victory, the crowd erupted. Children spilled onto the court and I attempted to make my way down there.

"That's my son!" I yelled to no one in particular. "That's my son!"

You spotted me and broke through the crowd, wielding a trophy in one hand. Smiling, you said, "You showed up."

"Of course, I did," I replied. "Fantastic job!"

Smirking, you looked at the trophy. "I'm sorry this isn't a hell of a report card instead."

I laughed and ruffled your hair and told you not to worry about it.

You smiled again and told me you would be going to Andre's, to pick you up from there in an hour.

I nodded and we departed, just like that.

An hour later, I approached the house. I rang the doorbell twice. No one answered so I knocked again and the door crept open. Confused, I stepped inside. I heard voices from upstairs so I walked up slowly. Thoughts racing through my mind, I heard some coughing and then your voice.

" . . . It gets so awkward sometimes, man."

"What do you mean?" That was Andre.

I got a little bit closer and saw the both of sitting in Andre's room. Something was in Andre's hand. I looked closer and realized what it was. It was a cigarette.

Then, Andre handed you it. Without hesitation, you took it out of his hand and inhaled.

After you blew the smoke out, you said, "We're so different, you know . . . me and him are two totally different people."

I was sure you were talking about me; part of me felt happy that I wasn't the only one that felt like that, part of me felt sad that it was like that.

You leaned in closer now and so did I, to hear you say, "It's like . . . if I didn't know better, I'd say I was adopted or some shit."

I hung my head in shame and headed back outside. Called you up and said I was here. As I stood by the car, looking at the sky, you walked outside. Your breath smelled of mints now. Clever.

"How was it?" I asked on the way home.

"It was good," you said and we rode home in silence.

———

"Wake up," I said. "We have to go pick up Kamal Uncle and his family."

It was a warm Sunday morning; your face was in the pillow and you refused to rise.

"No," you responded drowsily, pulling the sheets over you.

I rolled my eyes and groaned. I told you that Kamal had a daughter.

———

As we waited amongst the throng of people waiting to be reunited with their loved ones, you had countless questions. What's her name? How old is she? Is she smart? What does she like? What I noticed is that you were completely different toward females than you were toward anything else.

Your arrogant, masculine attitude vanished, and you were kind, sympathetic. Somehow, someway, you were a romantic inside.

I heard a voice calling my name to distract me from your myriad of questions. I turned and saw Kamal, standing there, clean-shaven, a bit chubby now but nothing too serious. As usual, he was smiling standing there with his wife and two kids. His daughter, Radhi had long black hair and light hazel eyes. Her skin was fair, and she glanced at you for a while then looked back down.

Ali was busy shaking my hand. He had grown up. His skin was blemish free; he had a handkerchief stowed in his chest pocket and a pair of black-rimmed glasses resting on his nose. His watch glistened in the lights above and he had dazzling white teeth.

"Salaam," he greeted me as he pushed his glasses back up his nose. He was dressed in a dress shirt that was tucked into dress pants. He had a certain aura of professionalism about him. He nodded at you and repeated the salutation; absentmindedly, you nodded back, your eyes fixed on Radhi.

Kamal came over and we hugged in a warm embrace.

"It has been too long," he said and I could feel him smiling.

I agreed with him and told him he could stay as long as he liked. As we began to depart, I asked Ali what he wished to pursue in terms of profession.

"Well," he began with a slight smirk, "I will probably go into medicine. Not exactly what I thought I would be doing, but hey, it'll bring the money in." He paused and then added, "I hear you're an excellent writer. I read all the time, perhaps you could show me what you've written once we arrive at your place?"

I was about to respond when I looked at you and you were making a barfing expression; I could already tell you weren't too fond of Ali.

I sighed and looked back at Ali and said, "Sure, no problem."

As we got into the car, Kamal sat in the front and Jamila and you and Radhi sat in the back. When there wasn't enough room for you, Ali got out and hailed a cab down. Got the address from me and smiled cheerily, saying it was no problem.

You got in the car with your eyebrows furrowed as we headed back home for dinner.

———

"No lie. I actually shook his hand. He gave me his number and told me to call him sometime, said we could go play cricket sometime. It was great."

Ali droned on and on about his meet and greet with a famous movie star Shahrukh Khan as you muttered words to Radhi and she muttered words back. Kamal and Jamila were oblivious; their eyes were fixed upon their prized possession, the fruit of the loom, their son.

"Ali is a great boy," Kamal would say proudly as he patted his son on the back. The conversation went on with Kamal asking you questions about school, what your hobbies were, and your interests. Your answers were always the same; bland, short, to the point. I began to ask Radhi questions, what she liked, what she wanted to be.

She loved music, she said. She liked to read and try new things. She said she wasn't sure what she wanted to be, but that she would probably become a doctor like her brother. She had brown eyes, shoulder-length black hair and a clear complexion.

As the dinner concluded, I announced the sleeping arrangements. Kamal and Jamila could have the guest room next to mine, you would let Ali sleep in your room and Radhi would get her own room in the basement.

Once everyone was settled in, I forgot that I hadn't checked the mail. As I slipped on my pajamas and stepped outside into the now familiar cool Chicago air, I walked toward the mailbox where I found a lone letter.

Taking it out and walking back to the house, I realized it was a letter from Aisha, Raiyah's sister in New York.

I sighed and wondered what she wanted this time.

As I sat on my bed and opened it, there were two pieces of paper. I picked the shortest one up first and read it out loud.

Faraz,

This is Raiyah's final message to you before she passed. You both lay next to each other in that hospital and while you were sedated, she wrote this to you.

I know it brings you pain but it is important that you read this.

All the best,
Aisha

Fingers trembling, I took it and put it to the side. I sighed and then picked up the other letter to see what Raiyah's final message was to me . . .

You always were the writer, Faraz. You were always the best at conveying your emotions, your thoughts, your feelings through your words.

You're screaming out words that should never even be uttered, "How can I love you if the pieces of my heart are too fragile to form?"

You taught me that love wasn't something to be afraid of. It is up to the believer to come across their destiny, their challenges, the choice to let out a sentiment so overpowering that it could devastate them . . . you taught me that to love somebody, you have to be strong.

You showed me that something broken can also be something beautiful, as to gaze at destruction and still see hope, or to look into a broken heart and still catch a glimmer of love.

I think of you from time to time; a lot actually. Your smile . . . I think of when you smiled, your whole face with a beautiful glow, as if the millions of fragments that surrounded you were smiling back. I think of your eyes, the most beautiful shade of brown I ever witnessed, a fascinating color that hypnotized me from the very beginning, the kind of eyes I could never forget.

They say that; "Absence makes the heart grow fonder" but it also makes the heart lonely, makes it suffer, bleed, hurt, die. I regret leaving for the "promised land" now. I should never have left you but I was young, ambitious . . . time doesn't wait Faraz and I needed something new. I must admit to you now . . . I did not feel the same passion with Ali as I did with you. Sure, he was successful, suave, sophisticated . . . but something was missing. I need you to know, Faraz, I need you to know that my love has never faltered; it could move mountains, travel over oceans, continents, and never get lost.

I remember reading something somewhere about what love really is. True love does not come by finding the perfect person, but learning to see an imperfect person perfectly. I see you perfectly, Rozzy.

I'm lying here on my deathbed and you're sedated in the bed next to me. Your chest rises and falls, rises and falls. I can't believe it's ending like this . . . they told me I wouldn't make it, Faraz.

Before I leave this world where the lone beacon of hope was you, I want to spread a message. I need to say something about love and what I've learned from it and how I wish everybody and nobody could experience such a feeling at the same time. The ironic thing about love is that, once you are in love . . . "I love you" doesn't even come close to accurately describing your feelings for your loved one.

So, I direct this to any person who can love without reason or doubt. If you come to a crossroad where you are being heartlessly estranged, having to start a new life apart yet still together. If there is any hesitation in your heart that you can't make it, then don't. Do not put yourself through an adverse inhumane pain that I feel no person should be put through; save yourself.

But, if you love, and are loved, then no distance should affect you, no ocean should be too wide, after all, those miles are only in your head, 3,000 is just a number, and remember, love can never be measured . . .

"Forever & Always"—do you remember that?
Raiyah

———

"Are you awake?"

There was a bustle at the door as you slowly crept into the basement, your shadow blending in with the still darkness of the room, your inconspicuousness aiding you. You see Radhi sitting on the bed, reading a book; *The Catcher in the Rye*.

"You're late," she said as you walked over and laid down on the floor, legs splayed and staring at the blank white ceiling.

"You really like reading, don't you?"

She nodded and smiled after that. Butterflies soared in your stomach, your heart skipped a beat, and you begin to perspire a bit but you didn't mind it; what was this feeling? Why was this happening?

She began to explain, "I read whenever I can . . . book is an escape from a world like this, you know?"

"Yeah, I know what you mean . . . I don't read much though," you said as you started observing her. Her hazel eyes, her perfect smile . . . you were only fourteen; you were only supposed to be concerned with hooking up with a girl once and then forgetting it, not experiencing this feeling . . .

You remembered what your friend Andre said when another friend of yours Nick felt bad because he was about to break up with his girlfriend. Andre spit on the ground and said, "Why are you such a pansy? Go ahead; break her heart. Who cares . . . she's just a girl, man."

"Fahad? Fahad?"

You snapped up immediately and started blushing, embarrassed.

"Sorry, I was thinking about something."

She laughed; she had the cutest laugh you had ever heard.

"So is your world perfect . . . you don't read?"

You chuckled a bit at that remark. I never heard this from you but your life was far from perfect.

"Not at all," you replied. You smiled and finished, "But I deal."

"That's good," she said with a pleasant tone and smiled again. She put the book by her side and pulled her knees up to her chest. Stared out the window looking for stars; she was always looking for stars, Radhi was.

"America seems so different to me," she said. Here she was, a Pakistani girl, thrust into the most industrialized country in the world, unaware of many customs, many traditions. You made a promise to yourself then, that you would help her in any way you could, you would try your best any chance you got . . .

She continued, "The real reason we're here is because of Ali and his stupid future."

You replied, "No offense, but your brother's a douche bag."

She laughed again. You loved it.

"Ali has his moments but he just wants to be successful. The only problem I have with him is that now I'm going to be forced to follow in his footsteps. I have no intention of going into medicine."

"Me neither!" you said, excited, thrilled that you had something in common with this girl other than your nationality.

She also seemed a bit relieved as she turned toward you now.

"I want to be a teacher when I grow up . . . the pay isn't good here in America but it's what I want to do. Unfortunately, I don't think it will happen."

You chose your words carefully, "Well, I mean, it's your life Radhi . . . you can do anything you want."

She smiled and said, "I wished it was that easy—another disadvantage of being Pakistani."

And so it began, a mountain of similarities and jokes and smiles and laughs between the two of you. Snide comments about the culture you both were raised in, discussions on parents, on love, on the future and what you hoped would happen one day for both of you. Radhi was in love with the idea of New York. She read all about it in Pakistan and it was her dream. You promised her that you'd take her there one day. She smiled and said you were sweet.

The days passed without words and the nights seemed to last forever with a myriad of laughs. There would be no communication between you and her during the day, I noticed, however at night I heard a faint noise in the basement and I wondered what would happen between the two of you, maybe you would fall in love at an early age like me or perhaps it would be a short term fling. Ali was busy with his career; he didn't pay you much attention and neither did his parents.

You had fallen for her, you truly had. There was no other way to describe it. I found it extremely ironic considering you seemed to loath everything to do with Pakistan and here you are, frolicking and laying out on the grassy lawn with Radhi, holding hands and staring at the star stricken sky.

She had enrolled at your high school now, roaming the hallways with you, smiling, laughing. She was always laughing with you, her eyes shimmering with delight, her face glowing once she saw you. I saw myself and Raiyah in the two of you and my only hope was that no obstacles come in your way; no problems appear in your path. However, what is true love without obstacles? That's what it comes down to . . . overcoming obstacles, facing any dilemma with a brave heart and a strong arm, knowing you each have the other to rely on no matter what.

Teasing ensued at first. Andre began to call you a "sellout", saying you had changed yourself for this girl which was far from the truth. Radhi had changed you. You had become more well mannered, you listened properly now, your grades rose. The downward spiral you were plunging into a few months back had now disappeared and you had climbed your way back up.

At night, both of you would go outside into the backyard and just lay there with each other, not a care in the world. It began to hit me that this was the first, true comparison between me and you, Fahad.

Radhi's parents didn't notice a thing. Pakistan had made them oblivious, made them naïve. They couldn't believe their daughter could be running around with a boy in the dark of the night, holding hands in public and always smiling when she was with you. They dismissed it as a simple euphoria; Jamila even went as far to call it a "phase".

Ali was also immersed in his studies; what did the medical student need to pay attention to his little sister's petty love affairs, he asked himself. In a few years, he would be a rich man, with an expensive car and luxurious house and he would have potential brides lining up at the door. He treated you like scum when I wasn't around, according to you; ordering you around in your own house, demanding the remote, and more rice, something to drink. Before you met Radhi, you would have confronted him and possibly injured him. But now, you smiled and did as you were told because you remembered what Radhi always told you; peace is the key to happiness.

Love is a funny thing though. It appears suddenly, rapidly, like a burst of flame or a massive inferno. It comes and goes without thought, without any time to process it; just enjoyment of what you have. In a flash, it seemed to fall apart. Radhi would become hesitant to spend time with you, sometimes going the other route at school, stating that she would walk herself to math class. You would be suspicious, but not too worried. You were fifteen and when someone tells you they love you at fifteen; you believe it.

It became awkward around the house. There were no more secret voyages out into the backyard for star gazing, no sly glances and giggles across the dinner table. She would eat quickly and excuse herself; you wouldn't eat a thing and continue pushing your food around your plate.

It broke my heart; it really did, when Ali finished school. Her parents said they were done here and it was time they find a place of their own. You said it wasn't fair. We said goodbye at the door one day and you headed upstairs to your room as soon as they left. I ate dinner by myself and left food by your door before I went to sleep. You were heartbroken, you felt cheated, deceived in every way.

I wanted to tell you I felt your pain, that I finally understood something about you. But the next morning, you no longer felt like discussing anything to do with her. Things went back to normal; your grades began to slip into mediocrity, you slouched around the house, you focused on basketball more than school. Radhi was your beacon of hope as Raiyah was mine. They both had improved us and then left us.

A few months passed and things had changed yet again. Sometimes, I guess, too much change can be a bad thing. My whole life, I've been looking for consistency, any way I can get it. That consistency never came, Fahad. I was troubled by thoughts of raising you, who your friends were, how Kamal was doing, if this was the right place for you and me, how Raiyah always kissed me on the nose before we slept. After all these years, I still feel the pain of her absence. There's been no other woman; I never loved anyone else. I know you laugh at that, you think it's absurd when I speak of her in such a way but at sixteen, what did you know? What does any sixteen year old know? You were busy embracing your liberty now, your freedom, driving around in the late hours of the night with Andre, coming home at 11 and crashing right away. Your license was a gift from heaven to you; it gave you a ticket out of the house, allowed you to leave whenever you wanted. You drove to school now, blasting your music in the driveway and wouldn't come home till 5 or 6. School got over at 3. You would say you went to the movies or went to get a bite to eat with some friends.

You were completely Americanized. You had transformed all of a sudden as you finally reached the elusive age of sixteen, eager to talk to girls and drive and be free. You were no longer the naive, love-stricken boy that had fallen head over heels for Radhi, whose name you barely remembered at times when I mentioned it. No, you came home with numbers of girls by the names of Emily, Jessie, and Rachel in your back pockets, which I would find when doing laundry. I would warn you about these girls, tell you to keep your focus on schoolwork and make sure you get to a good college; however, as all of my attempts regarding schoolwork with you were, they faltered.

You had begun to work out as well. Convinced me to pay a membership for you at a local gym where you went every weekend with Andre. Over the weeks, you had become toned. Your chest was chiseled and you had a spring in your step, a new found aura of arrogance seeping from your presence. You began to delve into school sports, claiming that basketball could not be your only sport; you joined the football team and, subsequently, the track team. You were a hell of a runner, I noticed at your meets. You sped through the tracks and paced yourself at the right times and you made it look so easy.

A faint scruff had begun to appear on your face and you embraced it wholeheartedly, trimming your facial hair and maintaining it. You were now built, looking older then sixteen, a tri-athlete and owned a car. Your voice had gotten deeper; authority poured out of your mouth when you spoke. You were a born leader amongst your friends.

One day, you asked if you could go to a party that your friend was having. Said you would be home at 11. I was busy that night anyway; I was meeting with a young author at the local coffee shop that my publishing company was looking at with interest, anyway. I said it was fine and you could go.

After you took off in your car, I found a letter in your room. While cleaning, I resisted the urge to pick it up and read it. When I was done and was about to leave the room, I couldn't resist. I turned around and opened it up, my eyes squinting.

—

:) ♥♥♥♥♥♥ Fahad ! I'm throwin' down this weekend at my place and i reallllllllly want you to come. Try your best . . . you won't regret it, I promise.

I loooooooooooove you!

love, Jessie :)

—

Feeling a lot of emotions all at once, I wondered who this girl was and how far would she take you? My god, you were only sixteen; I couldn't imagine you having sex at such an age. Then, I remembered myself, falling for Raiyah at the same age and the last thing I wanted to be back then was a hypocrite. I figured you would come home and everything would be fine.

I'm starting to wonder how many times I can be wrong.

It rained hard that night, the windows covered with water, the constant spattering against the panes. It was an hour later. You had not come home yet and I was pacing the room. What had happened? You had not picked up your phone. Did you get in some sort of trouble?

As soon as that last thought left my mind, the doorbell rang and I ran toward it, slinging it open. There you were, completely drenched and face down. The door opened a little more and there was a police officer. It was then that I noticed you were in handcuffs. For a second, I couldn't breathe.

"Sir? Sir?"

The cop was talking to me but all I could focus on was your posture, eyes fixed on the wet, gray asphalt right outside our home.

"Sir, is this your son?"

I gulped and then nodded, still not believing, still not wanting to believe.

The cop sighed and began, "Sir, your son was pulled over at 10:17 today. He was driving recklessly and ran quite a few red lights. While I understand that he just turned sixteen, such driving can be expected and tolerated with. However, once we pulled him over, we did a test on him and his blood alcohol level was two times the limit. We also found an ounce of marijuana in the car."

This information was hitting me like a wave. This was it. You had become a drug addict, a drunk, a menace to society. The cop kept talking, but I had zoned out. All I thought about was how lucky you were to be alive that night and that if I lost you that night, I didn't know what I would have done.

The officer concluded, "I confiscated the drugs and took him here where he said he lives. I'm not putting this on the record because kids make mistakes but I assure you, sir, if this happens again, your son will have to deal with the consequences."

He said goodnight and walked back to his police cruiser while you stepped into the house. I closed the door gently and silence ensued. You grabbed a towel and began to dry yourself off.

"How could you?" I blurted, angry with you.

"Dad . . ." you said.

"Don't 'Dad' me. Are you serious right now? You drank at that party and got behind that car? What if you died tonight, Fahad? Did you think about that?"

You were quiet and headed upstairs to your room and slammed the door.

I sat on the couch and listened to the rain pelt the window panes—drop after drop. I didn't know what to do with you anymore.

I called Kamal and asked him if he would like to drive down next weekend for the holidays. He said he'd like that. I told him to bring the whole family. If I can't help this kid, I wondered, maybe Radhi can.

The sun shone with an unusually bright glow that day, dazzling rays of light blinding those stuck in traffic. Cars were piling up in the freeway, all eager to leave the windy city and go on vacation to somewhere warm and pleasant, Miami, maybe. Large, white, ominous clouds drifted overhead and hid the sun from view sporadically. Somewhere, a pastor was preaching to his church about the evils of the world and somewhere, a pick-up game of basketball was being played in the hot sun with vulgarities flying left and right. And somewhere, a car was pulling into a driveway, a driveway stained with pessimism and tension.

They were here for the holidays, the spring air pungent with happiness and joy, washed over them as they stepped out of the car and headed up the stairs to knock on the door.

You were laying on the couch with a bowl of cereal, laughing at Tom and Jerry, clad in your King Kong pajamas and favorite grey hoodie. Laughing, you heard the doorbell ring. It rang again and you mustered the strength to get up and walk to the door. Checking yourself in the mirror, you opened the door and you came to face with Radhi.

Your heart skipped a beat. She had grown up, to put it simply. Her light hazel eyes and affable smile with perfect white teeth still sent your heart into euphoria; it felt as if it were running laps around your body. Her perfect, unblemished brown skin was perfect and fair in the light, her clear complexion taking your breath away. She was wearing a white summer dress that went down to right below her knees complete with white flip flops. Her black hair fell elegantly over her back as she tucked a strand of it behind her ear.

"Looking a bit sloppy, Fahds." And she smiled and laughed and your heart burst into flames, happiness soared through your body and your face grew red as you stepped forward and asked, "Why are you here?"

She frowned for a second then smiled.

"Why?" She said suggestively, taking a step toward the door. "You want me to leave?"

"No," you said a little too quickly. Her eyebrows raised at this and smirked.

"Your dad invited me and my dad here," she said.

Before you had a chance to register what was happening, you felt a hand on your shoulder. It was me.

"Fahad, you remember Radhi, don't you?"

You nodded slowly, your smile forming as Kamal stepped in with a suitcase and said his salaam.

I continued, "They will be staying with us for spring break."

You glanced at me and glanced back at Radhi.

"Where's Ali?" you asked; I had been waiting for the question.

Kamal answered, "Ali is busy with school. He said he would stay at his college for break, insisted we come alone." Kamal shrugged, suddenly embarrassed for some reason.

I said it was no problem, knowing you were reveling in the fact he wouldn't be here.

Later that night, when all had slept, you fell into an old pattern. Escaping the comfort of your room, you sneaked downstairs stealthily into the basement, where she was waiting for you, her feet dangling over the edge of the bed, her black hair blending in with her background.

You walked in and she smiled.

"It's been a while, hm?" She asked a twinkle in her eye.

You laughed and rubbed the back of your head. "Yeah, you could say that."

You sat on the floor and continued, "So much has happened since you left."

Her eyebrows rose as she proceeded to join you on the floor, her hand on your arm, her breath hot on you.

She asked you to explain then and you looked at her, grateful for a chance to let it all out to somebody. You began to chronicle your adventures since she left all the way up to your drunken escapade through the streets of Chicago. You left the part out about you having a girlfriend though—Jessie.

She listened intently. She was perfect at it. She gasped at the right moments, laughed when it was needed and placed a comforting hand on you when she knew you needed it.

When you were done, she said, "Well . . . at least my brother's not here."

You chuckled at that and she smiled. The two of you began to talk about everything and nothing, walking around the room playing games, impersonating Ali and making jokes that only the two of you would find funny.

Two hours had passed and your jaw hurt from smiling and your throat from laughing. Knowing you had to whisper; you leaned in slowly to see her beaming face, filled with joy and whispered, "Radhi?"

"Yeah?"

She smiled and you moved a bit more forward and kissed her. She was taken aback at first but kissed you back as you lay on the floor there, connected by lips and love; everything yet nothing. You remembered that her lips tasted like strawberry, loving it, reveling in it.

When you were done, you both sat next to each other, panting heavily and looking at each other.

"I missed you," was all you could say.

"I want to tell you something," she said.

When you didn't say anything, she continued, "Okay . . . silly little fantasy I had of calling you up and it goes really well and I confess to writing you all these love letters . . ."

You interrupted, "Love letters?"

She changed pace, quipped, "More like fuck love letters."

You observed her for a few seconds and asked, "So . . . no love letters?"

Radhi smiled for a second and said, "Well, yeah . . . some love letters."

You straightened up and said, "Good."

And, suddenly, Radhi is impossibly happy, heart swelling up and bursting over into flames.

Amidst her joy, she hears you whisper distantly, "I'm so glad you came. It means . . . the world to me."

—

Time, like everything else, passes and leaves us confused, wondering whatever happened to that one person or why we've arrived here and are not there. It can last a lifetime or a second but it is always moving, not stopping so you can relive those memories whenever you want or talk to that person whenever you feel like it.

Time didn't wait for you. Spring break flew by, and Radhi had packed her bags and was waiting for her father by the door, yet again. You watched helplessly as she left, your heart pounding, but you didn't say anything. You would tell me years later, if you had just said something, anything, things might have changed and it would not be like it is now between the two of you. You would no longer avoid each other and shy away from talks of nostalgia and childhood memories. Damn, all you could do was stand there and watch Kamal walk down the stairs, his beard now with several patches of gray; he always told me America had taken its toll on him and his traditional ways.

Kamal had withered over the years. He had developed arthritis recently and the thing that irked him the most was not that he could not be as active as he was before or that he had to ask to have something given to him. It was that he could not complete his prayer and had to pray from a chair; he called himself pitiful and that he was ashamed. Can you imagine that? He was suffering from a chronic disease and all he was concerned about was that he could not complete *salat* the right way, the precise way. I told him that God wouldn't mind, He excuses illness, but Kamal said he thinks he developed this disease because God wanted him and expected him to fight through it.

I'll never forget the one day he came downstairs, his eyes red; he had been weeping for a while. I was busy working on a manuscript when I heard his sandals tap the wooden floor and with his frequent coughing and wheezing make his way toward me. I turned and saw him and God, he was broken down. His hair was disheveled and his glasses were missing. He just sat on the chair next to me and started crying again. I don't think I told you about this incident, but it broke me, Fahad. Kamal was my childhood friend, the one that never left my side or abandoned me, that always helped me in my time of need. I looked up to him and sought his advice on any problems I had. And now, he was in my house crying and talking about it was a mistake to leave Pakistan and come to America. He said he had brought shame to his family and shame to his country. I patted him on the back and told him it would be okay, because what else was I supposed to say? Then he dropped the bomb; his brother had just called from Karachi telling him the people that conceived both of them just died in a roadside bomb.

He had to get out of there. He felt like a phony, an ungrateful man who had left his family there to die. His words stung me; I had been like that but I didn't feel half the pain my best friend felt. He said he was leaving in the morning, him and Radhi. They would go to NYC and get Ali and depart to Pakistan; just get away for a while.

Radhi stood with her bags ready and packed and Kamal walked down the stairs for the last time. He shook my hand goodbye and then looked at you for a moment or two.

"Jeetey raho." Stay right.

He left the house then straight to the airport. I would see Radhi again; as would you, but the both of us never saw the most honorable man I knew ever again.

—

"Fahad has evolved into a fine young man. His attitude, his grades; everything has dramatically improved. I'm not sure where his motivation came from, Mr. Ahmad, but your son has a great shot for most colleges."

We were having the end of year meeting with the college counselor, the principal, the senior and the parent. You beamed as Mr. Holloway continued to compliment you, calling your effort "exceptional" and your attitude "heartwarming." You had grown taller now; maybe 5 foot 10 inches, possibly 11. You kept the goatee but refused to have long hair anymore; you kept it short. You would no longer don basketball jerseys and white tees everyday; you wore dress shirts more often and kept everything organized. You had grown up, as I knew you would. I knew it, Fahad.

We shook hands with both of the men and stood. Thanked them for their time. As we left, you said, "Babaji, I can't wait for college."

In my mind, I thought, I can. But to you, I said, "I know."

I wasn't ready to let you go just then. You would delve out into the world, like a bird released from a cage and inhibit yourself in the realities of the world, exposing your newfound innocence to a world anything but; you had not smoked or drank in two years.

I had grown old over the years too, sorry to say. I had a balding spot you would tease me about, offering me your hats whenever we went out. I had lived such a prosperous yet troublesome life. But I could not completely wallow in misery now. I loved Raiyah, but I see her every day in you, Fahad. You are the noor of my eyes, the rose of my garden. You were the only thing I had and sometimes I wish we didn't go home that day, that we had stopped somewhere else or some red lights caused us to wait five more minutes, if it did, maybe you would talk to me, you would come visit me. I wronged you, I realize, but I keep thinking, maybe . . . just maybe . . .

But I met my shame that night; the past always comes back to haunt you. You can forget it all you want but it still happened. I still lied to you for eighteen years. And for that, I pray this finds you in good health, and you can find it in your heart to come visit your father and knock on my door. I will be old, I will be ailing. But I will answer, and I will take you and your family in, grant you true acceptance, as I always have and weep until my eyes fall out. I pray, I pray, Fahad, you find me in my house here in this lonely suburb and return to your childhood. I will be waiting.

What happened next pains me to death. I'll never forget what happened or the look on your face as you came to realization or the look on their faces, those who had flown over the seas to come get what is theirs. It may be hard to understand, Fahad, but what happens in one day, maybe even in a couple of hours, can change the course of an entire lifetime.

He had the same color eyes as well. His posture was shabby; he looked like he had been through hell and back. The woman was smiling; she always smiled. They were standing outside of our house, perplexed, looking nervous, anxious.

You noticed them first.

"Who are those people outside of our house, Babaji?"

I shrugged but a sour feeling formed in my stomach. We pulled into the driveway and the couple turned around, resting their eyes on you and I.

I got out first and asked, "Forgive me, but who are you?"

The two looked at you then at each other then at me. The man replied, "Could we speak to you inside, sir?"

I nodded nervously and led them inside. As I looked back, I noticed the woman's eyes were locked onto you. My stomach flipped. It was then I knew.

We sat on the couches, sipping cups of tea. The man took one sip and put the cup down.

"My name is Bilal," he began. "This is my wife, Hina. We have traveled here from Pakistan. It took several phone calls, a handful of inquiries but we made it here."

"What's your business here?"

The man nodded at you and my heart plummeted.

"I understand that you have lived with this boy for the past eighteen years. Nurtured him, fathered him, and taught him the morals and standards expected out of a human being."

I nodded and replied, "I tried my best."

The man continued talking but he was looking at you. "I hope you understand what I am about to tell you, sahib. With all due respect . . . well, I don't know how to word this. But this boy is mine."

This boy is mine. Four words, two seconds. That's all it took to shatter two lives at once.

You stood, as did I. You beat me to it.

"What the hell are you talking about man? We don't even know who the hell you are!"

The man continued, "You know who I am, Rafiq. You just don't know who I am and maybe that's my fault."

Hina stood now and said something before I could, "I only held you once, God forgive me, and I only held you once."

You backed up, hitting tables, knocking the drinks over.

"I'm your father, Rafiq," the man said gently. "You were adopted and lied to for the past eighteen years. This man swooped into Pakistan and plucked you out of the orphanage we left you in two days earlier. Then he scrambled back to America and he didn't even bother to . . ."

"Shut the fuck up!" You were yelling. "All of you just shut the fuck up! What the fuck is going on?" You looked at me and repeated yourself.

The woman was crying now. "Rafiq, please, oh God, forgive me, and forgive me . . ."

Bilal turned to me and said, "I think you should tell my son the truth, sahib. Tell him what you've hidden from him all these years." Then he did something that damn near killed me; he pulled out a birth certificate and placed it on the table.

Rafiq J. Azam, son of Bilal and Hina Azam.

My heart was pounding. I couldn't breathe, couldn't function.

You looked to me now. Without asking, you saw it in my eyes.

"It's true, isn't it? That's why we're nothing alike, I never came out of any woman named Raiyah, I never held her hand, you fucking liar! How could you do something like this! What the fuck were you thinking?"

I didn't say anything. Nothing I would say that night would change your mind. You didn't wait for me to say anything, either. You grabbed the birth certificate and ran out of the house. Bilal and Hina ran after you and, just like that, I was alone.

Life changes for all of us.

It changed for Kamal when he fell ill attending the funeral of his parents, when Radhi became his caretaker, and Ali just couldn't miss his meetings to visit an ailing father. My mind flashed back to the scene at the dinner table when I heard the news. Kamal ruffling his then humble son's hair, calling himself a "proud father" and Ali an "enigma." I almost puked when I thought about it. He left his family behind when he became successful and never looked back. Most give back as I expected you too. Now Kamal is no longer a part of this world and Ali regretted it; regretted when it was too late.

It changed for Faizan when a father he barely knew showed up at his door step; arms wide open, begging for repentance, for forgiveness. Amin sought atonement; there were nights he could not bear Faizan's gradual acceptance and came to me weeping, "I don't deserve what he's given me, Faraz." But we all make mistakes don't we? It's human nature. Dwelling in the past will not reverse bad deeds. It was time for him to move on and bask in his sunshine, be grateful to Allah his son has shown such mercy and such companionship, when, to be frank, no one thought Amin deserved it.

It changed for Raiyah when she found opportunity in America, her ambition leading her overseas, her beautiful green eyes scanning the American horizon, resting on the Statue of Liberty, telling me one day Pakistan will have its own Statue of Liberty. I laughed at her, her dreams, her ambition but now I feel envious, wishing I could have the same kind of vision. When the news came her father passed, a father she hated—but a father. I still feel the sting of her palm on my cheek, Fahad. Call me crazy, and I know it would hurt like hell, but I would give anything to have her slap me again just so I could feel her touch.

And it changed for me when you took off that day. I had gone through so much; I couldn't take it. When I received a letter from you saying you needed some time to clear your head and would be back in a week, I knew what I had to do. I packed my bags and was on my way to Pakistan to get some answers.

I left the house with a note attached to the front door in case you came back. You didn't come back, I should have known, but I left that note there anyway. I boarded the flight feeling frightful, nervous. The thing that scared me the most was how much Pakistan had changed after all these years. It scared me to death, honestly. As the plane began to take off, I gripped the armrest. Plenty of things had changed but after all these years, I still hated flying.

A few minutes into the air, I leaned back and dozed off.

There is an old building. Crows have gathered together as a pack on the top of it, cawing away into the dirt filled atmosphere. A car stops in front of the building and a couple steps out; the woman is holding a baby. They proceed to enter the building when they are attacked by a man. He knocks the man down and takes the child when the woman is surprised. Turns around and puts the child in the car and drives off. He is laughing. While he is adjusting the rearview mirror and sees the woman crying in the background, I wake up in a cold sweat with everyone looking right at me.

The man in the car was me.

———

I arrived at Kamal's place first. Offered my condolences and brought some flowers. Radhi greeted me with open arms, asking me what I was doing here, if you had come with me. God, just hearing your name now was like a slap to the face. She asked more about you; she was so curious. You both had grown up; Radhi was going to end up a lawyer as were her father's last wishes if she refused to partake in medical school. She asked what you had decided as your profession and when I didn't answer, she knew something was wrong.

Ali just sat around, wallowing; either on the couch with his face in his hands or on the balcony, staring out into the dusty horizon of Karachi, the smell of kabobs and gasoline filling the atmosphere. It had affected him more than anything. His father had called for him in his last moments, Radhi told me. Kamal had wailed and wailed but there was no Ali.

We sat down on the couch, Radhi and I. I took one sip of the tea she brewed and then couldn't take it anymore. I began to rant—tell her everything—about Raiyah, about her last wish, about the adoption, about the arguments and the fights, about the relationship between you and her, and how I rarely saw him that happy with a girl, about 9/11, about that goddamned Bilal and his wife.

And then, all of a sudden, when I finished my story, I began to laugh. I was hysterical. Then the tears came. Then I was laughing and crying at the same time. I don't know; I just felt so pure. I felt cleansed, relieved that someone finally knew me for who I really was.

Radhi was silent. Then a tear fell.

I asked her to come with me to America. There was nothing she could do for Kamal anymore. But she could do something for her father's best friend.

She was quiet and didn't say anything.

Later on, I was praying Maghrib; I had taken up praying more often lately. I noticed her approach, but she waited for me to finish. When I was done, I turned my head and saw her straighten up and say, "I'll come with you—Ali as well."

"Thank you, thank you, thank you!" I said and broke down.

After convincing Ali and Radhi to accompany me to America, my next stop was the orphanage—the place where it all began. Ali offered to come with me; the poor soul was desperately seeking for any kind of redemption or atonement. In any other case, I would let him but this; this was something I had to settle on my own.

I exited the house and called for a cab. A burly man with thick chest hair and a constant sheen of sweat on his forehead stopped and opened the door for me. He had a couple of gold bracelets on his left wrist; they could be spotted as counterfeit miles away. I told him I wished to go to the orphanage in Peshawar. I was looking for the owner. The man rubbed his hand across his forehead and chuckled.

"My friend," he began, "Which lucky child do you wish to bring back to America with you?"

I suddenly felt uncomfortable as the truth hit me; I was an outsider here after having been gone so long. I had acquired an American accent and had Western behavior that I had assimilated, and I was being blamed for it. But I was done backing down.

"I'm not here to take a child," I responded, your name flashing in my mind. "I'm here to get some answers."

The man "tsked" again and coughed a couple times. He really was a dirtbag.

He ignored me and asked, "So tell me about America . . . how is that whore these days?"

I became more and more uncomfortable with each passing word. A red light appeared and he cocked his head back and looked at me. His eyes were bloodshot and he had plenty of acne. Grease ran through his hair. Did I mention he was a dirtbag?

"Wah, wah!" he said, putting both hands in the air with feigned surprise, "Americans don't think anyone is worthy to talk to?"

I ignored him and said, "Please hurry to the orphanage."

He stared at me intently and turned around, muttering something. He didn't say a word till we got to the building in my dreams.

He screeched to a halt and demanded twenty rupees. The counter said 10. Foreigner Tax, the bastard said.

I paid him his goddamn money and walked out of the taxi feeling like a felon. Shaking the feeling off, I walked inside the orphanage and noticed how tattered the place had become. It was bad to begin with; but the place you knew first had become garbage. I walked through the throng of children and knocked on the door to the single closed room. The owner opened it, smiling. His smile quickly turned to a frown.

"Faraz sahib . . . after all this time?"

I lost it.

I lunged at him, knocked his face in, kicked him, smashed his glasses . . . I was in a frenzy. It went on like that for a minute until he wheezed, "The children, sahib . . . the children."

Breathing heavily, I looked back and saw all of them frozen, staring at us. One little girl was crying.

Faisal stood slowly and spit some blood out into his handkerchief; beckoned me inside and closed the door.

I apologized first and told him my story; about you, about Bilal. He closed his eyes, as if he was trying to remember and then he opened them.

"I remember that day," he said, staring right past me into the wall. "They were a sweet couple, they were." He paused. "Do you want to know their story?"

I was quiet and then I nodded.

Faisal took a sip of his tea, leaned his head against the wall, and spoke.

They walked in on a rainy day. Hina's eyes were red; she'd been weeping. Bilal was resilient and stared me in the rye, handed me a one-year-old baby and said they couldn't take care of it anymore. Said it was called Rafiq. You're wondering why I told you it was called Fahad; well, it's because it's all the child responded to as a young one. At the name Rafiq, he would sit and stare off but at Fahad, he would instantly become alert and look at the source of the noise, laughing. I never understood.

Anyway, I invited both of them into my office and they both took a seat, Hina was not looking up. Bilal said they were planning to run away;

they were madly in love—maybe to India then America, he said with a bitter sweet smile. But they could not take the child with them. They did not have enough money and he would die on the streets. He told me he would back; he swore on his mother's grave that he would be back for him and his lover's child. I agreed to keep him; I looked that man in the eye and said that I promised to keep him. He thanked me over and over, kissed my hand, said I was an honorable man and he was proud to know me.

I was greedy and foolish. Two days after they left, you walk in the door. It was destiny, maybe and god's will. The Lord works in strange ways, Faraz, and hopefully someday you'll understand.

I was broke. I needed money. You walked in and almost automatically, this boy and you had some sort of connection, some bond. I couldn't believe it. So here I was, a son who's shamed his own father, who buried his own mother at fourteen and with only a couple of dollars to his name, and I gave in. I took the money from you and let you adopt him. I lived in fear for the next couple of days and the most terrible thoughts ran through my head. Running away was a serious crime; what if they had gotten caught? Surely at that time they would've been executed. But they didn't.

The two of them came here a week ago, looking for their son. I couldn't believe my eyes. Bilal was a sturdy man with a handsome smile and thick hair, a sharp-looking fellow. Hair slicked back, dashing white teeth, broad shoulders. Hina was exceptionally pretty with hazel eyes and an affable twinkle in them.

And I didn't have their child. So what did I do? I gave them your name, sahib. I pray you forgive me; I pray Allah forgives me because I have led a pitiful life. I have done nothing good to help anyone; I have not assisted anyone in their time of need. God, if you had just seen the look on Hina's face when I told her son was in a city she had never even heard of in her life . . . if only you had seen it, sahib.

I pray you forgive me. I pray that in return for your forgiveness, your boy forgives you and makes the right decision. Go back to America and be with your son. He is your son, sahib. You have cared for him all your life; he will not betray you in your time of need.

———

Faisal finished and I was sitting there with a numb mind. I thanked him for his kindness, his generosity. I told him I forgave him and apologized for my blows. They would heal, he said; his honor would not.

I left the building with a newfound sense of confidence. I returned to Kamal's and left with Radhi and Ali. This would be my third time leaving my homeland, I realized as I boarded the plane and closed my eyes. And it would be my last.

—

EPILOGUE

[one month later]

Fahad's POV

I put the letter down. Sigh.

"I pray this finds you in good health and you can find it in your heart to come visit your father and knock on my door," he wrote.

I am living alone now. I did not want to face Bilal and Hina; as far as I am concerned, they were never my parents. A birth certificate doesn't mean anything if they didn't even hold me, right? But then again, I lived with a man who lied to me shamelessly year after year after year. Who am I? Rafiq? Fahad? Do I have a name? My identity has been stolen; it has been snatched up and ripped into pieces and thrown into the wind.

But I missed it. I missed the nights with him, impersonating Faizan, impersonating Ali. God, I'm thinking about Radhi now. I promised myself I wouldn't, I swear I did, but I was thinking about her, about her smile and the way her eyes seem to radiate light.

I knew I had to make a decision soon. He must be miserable, right? Gone are the days when I knew who I was; I am no one.

"I have to get out of this apartment," I said to no one in particular when fate reared its head and knocked on my door.

I froze. I never had visitors. I didn't tell anyone where I was . . . except . . .

I went to open the door and there was the most beautiful girl I've ever known. She had not changed yet she had. Her light hazel eyes melted me right away. She smiled; her teeth perfectly white and she tucked a strand of loose hair behind her ear and still smiling.

She looked at me knowingly. "Are you going to invite me in?" she asked.

I stepped to the side and she strolled in, dodging the clothes lying around on the floor. As she passed by, I caught a whiff of still strawberries.

You look great," I blurted as she made her way through the apartment.

She sat on the couch. "Thanks, Fahad," Radhi laughed nervously. "You've really let go of this place, haven't you?"

I ran a hand through my hair and nodded sheepishly.

"What are you doing here?" I asked even though I knew exactly what she was doing here.

I was right. She looked at me with a knowing look and said, "I think you know."

I did know. She told me that Faraz is in ruins; he sits on the rocking chair on the porch, each and every day, from 8 AM to 8 PM and waits for me. That he won't eat, he won't sleep; he becomes frustrated easily.

"Life changes, Radhi," I said. "He lied to me for years."

"Some things do change," she said. "Like you and me. We can fix that. I want to fix that, Fahad. Just like I know you want to fix things with your father."

I was quiet, and she asked where Bilal and Hina were. I told her I didn't know and didn't care; I didn't want to see or meet anyone.

"Faraz was in ruins, Fahad," she told me. "I know what he did wasn't fair. Not to you, not to Bilal and Hina but you have to see where he's coming from, Fahad. He didn't wish to cause you any trouble, any harm. He was ailing at the time; coming off the death of a wife, her last wishes spiraling around in his mind and also the death of his father; again, he was in ruins."

"I don't know," was all I said. Stood and walked over to the fridge and opened a bottle of beer.

"You drink now?" She asked softly.

"Lightly," I replied and chugged it.

"It's 2 in the afternoon, Fahad."

I shrugged and said, "Really, why are you here? Why don't you go off to your brother and bask in his money?"

"Because, I care about you, Fah . . ."

"Hah!" I laughed. "Well I don't care about you! Why should I? Last time I cared about anyone else, I damned myself."

"You don't mean that," she said.

"How do you know? You were just a girl I met here and there; we never really had anything concrete!"

As soon as it dawned on me what I said, I felt a pang of remorse. But I didn't feel like stopping. I had to get angry at someone.

"Just a girl," she repeated out loud. "You told me I was anything but, you used to tell me when it was you and me, nobody else mattered, you used to talk to me like I was the only one around, you used to . . ."

"My life has been flipped upside down, Radhi! What are you not understanding! We're not kids anymore, we can't say everything's going to be alright anymore like we always did, we can't be so fucking optimistic like we always were, I can't be with you like I was and I can't be there for you either . . . I just can't do it."

I got the hell out of that apartment and called for a cab. Told him to go anywhere; it didn't matter. As we pulled away, I saw Radhi walking down the steps and for the first time in my life I started to cry.

———

"Please remember to come to the fund-raiser for the masjid tonight and to donate some money on your way out. Allah bless you all," the imam finished.

Faraz lingered after everyone was gone. He approached the imam.

"Do you have a moment, sahib?"

The man nodded and beckoned Faraz into his office.

When he finished telling his story, the imam sighed. Put his hands together, took his glasses off and stroked his beard.

"Faraz sahib, you have done an honorable thing. You took an abandoned child in and cared for him. However, you have not been honest, and Allah looks down upon such as you certainly know," the imam began.

"I know but . . ."

"If you are right in your description of this child, he will come back. He will come back and you should be ready to stand there with open arms and a warm heart because that's all he will need. God is unhappy with you right now, Faraz sahib, but he forgives and he always shall; remember, it is to him we shall return so I will pray tonight that you shall return to him along with your boy."

Faraz shook the man's hand and thanked him over and over again. As he was leaving the masjid, he saw some boys playing basketball. A boy went up and shot a fifteen-foot shot from the right side. Swish.

Fahad's game winner.

—

Dear Fahad,

I don't know where you are or if this letter will find you. I am sending it to where Radhi has told me you are staying, in some dingy apartment downtown. You don't have to do this, you know. I hope you realize someday that I made a mistake but understand my heart bleeds for you; it cries and it weeps. It's longing for you to return, to forgive.

Radhi has told me she has seen you. You yelled at her, told her to leave. Is this how you want it to end? I remember you telling me you wanted to marry her, Fahad. I remembered dreaming of you and her with kids and that we both would finally have some sort of family. I ask you, I beg you don't let me leave this world without anybody. Being strong is important, Fahad, but knowing who you can count on is equally important. It's a sad thing when people you know become people you knew. When I can walk right past you, like you were never a part of my life. How we lived under the same roof for years and now, now I don't think I could bear to look you in the face.

Something is missing. I don't know what, but I can feel it. I mean, I can really feel it. I can feel your anger, your sorrow all the way from here. It kills me. It really does.

I'm not sure what else to say to you. I realize that it is extremely difficult for you to read this and feel sympathy for me . . . but I have no one. You're all I've got. I just . . . I know you're forgetting about me and there's nothing I can do about it. You will go to college, you will be successful, you will be wealthy and you won't look back. You will have started a new life: Meet a new girl, leave Radhi in the dust, and start a family and have dinner parties without me. There will be no grandpa, and when your children ask why they don't have one, you will not shiver, you will not hesitate. You will say "because" and you will go to attend to the kitchen or the grill. Your heart will not break, your mind will not be filled with images of me, of Radhi; you will have a cleared conscious and you won't return. But, as I told you, I will be sitting. I will be waiting. Waiting with open arms, praying that he grants me this last wish, that I get to lay my eyes on you once more, even if for a second. In my quest to fulfill Raiyah's last wish, I have failed. I am a broken man, Fahad and you are the final straw.

I'm getting old. My arthritis has kicked in; I take pills every day, and Radhi helps me into the bed. But she has to move on. She will not be with me forever. She will leave, and she will not be my daughter-in-law; she will be one of the few at my funeral to acknowledge this pitiful life I've led, full of lies and deceit. If you don't come visit me, please find it in your heart to come to my funeral. I don't have much longer to live. I really don't. I hope you find it in you to come say a few words at your father's funeral. It is a dying man's wish. Save me from this misery; you are the vaccine to my disease. You are the noor of my eyes; the rose of my garden. The Dalai Lama once said "Take into account that great love and great achievements involve great risk." I guess the risk has finally caught up to me . . .

All the best,
Faraz

Fahad,

You acted like you didn't know who I was yesterday when I visited you. Don't you remember? Those late nights, those claims of us being forever together, those stupid jokes, the stargazing?

I love you. That's my secret. No hearts. No pretty drawings. No poems or cryptic messages. I love you.

You loved me too. I remember hearing your voice in my ear, saying it, promising me you wouldn't leave. I believed you . . . at sixteen, I believed you. You make me want a time machine. I don't know why I'm writing this, I don't think I'm making sense; I mean, I don't know, won't you come have dinner with me some night? Won't you give me the time of day? Won't you? The world's falling down around me . . . won't you be my constant? Be my home, my second half?

You made me feel safe. You fueled my spirit yet you understood my soul. Like our bodies, our insecurities . . . are just jigsaws falling into place. You've endured so much. But now . . . I love you, Fahad. At least I used to love you—very loving, yet so utterly blind. You were great to me. You were good to you. You're horrible to us. You made me hate myself. You made me hate you. You made me regret us.

Nobody has made me feel the way you made me feel. That dorky smile, those green eyes, that messy black hair . . . you were a dream. I'm just so afraid . . . afraid I'll never move on and find somebody else.

Faraz is getting ill. He's coughing blood and he moans your name in his sleep. All I can do is cry and tell him it will be okay. But he really needs you. I need you. I hope you come back, Fahad, and end this nightmare.

You always told me I was the smartest girl in the world; the prettiest, the funniest. You told me I could conquer everything . . . well it looks like I can't conquer you. I should have told you all of this long ago. Maybe you wouldn't have reacted this way, maybe you would get out of that apartment and clean yourself up and become a part of my life again. Become a part of your father's life. He is waiting, Fahad but when it is too late, don't blame me. Don't blame him. Blame yourself. He sits on that porch everyday. I ask him if he's hungry and he says he will wait for you to return from the courts. "Faraz Kaka," I say, "Fahad's not here." He'll look at me like I was the crazy one. Nonsense, he would say with a wave of his hand. Said you'd be back in five minutes. That you were just shooting around, probably about to hit a game winner.

You should come home. Maybe we can patch things up. Be like we used to. Everything can be the same again, Fahad . . . good-bye can also be a second chance. I suggest you take it.

With love,
Radhi

Hey man,

Wow. I can't even imagine what you're going through, bro. I know we don't get along that well; we basically never did, but know that I'm here for you man. My dad only came back a while ago. I hated him—hated him before I even knew the guy. Imagine that? But I forgave him, man. It took a while. It really did. But I forgave him. I hope you do too.

Later,
Faizan

Fahad,

Forgive.

Sincerely,
Ridah & Amin

—

To the shadows of my past,

You are all too much. One thing you have to understand about me is that I'm still in shock. I can't believe it. I simply can't. Sure, I miss it, but I feel that if I go back now and am with all of you, that I'd be living a lie. Maybe I'll come back soon. Get my head straight, clear my heart. I miss you, Radhi, especially. I'm sorry I lashed out at you like that. I didn't mean what I said . . . you should know that. To Faizan and your parents, I appreciate your concern and I will consider it. And for . . . Faraz, I miss you. Like really. But I can't come back now . . . I just can't.

I'm planning on going to college. I'll return during one of the holidays. Just be ready for my return and by then, I will be ready to sit down and talk it over. I will be ready to be with you all again, I will hold hands with you Radhi and we'll go back to our teenage years, I will overcome my differences with Faizan and for you, Faraz, I will embrace you and forgive you for what you've done. It was not your fault; you needed something. You couldn't tell me. It would break me. You were right. You are a real hero. The real hero is always a hero by mistake; he dreams of being an honest coward like everyone else.

While it pains me to be away for so long, you must realize I have no other choice. It is the principle of things . . . it would not be right to act like nothing has changed, like nothing happened. Maybe things will work out, maybe we'll be sitting at a dinner table, laughing and talking or we'd all go our separate ways and never see each other again. I just . . . I know there must be something more.

Please don't try to find me. It is my last request of you. When the time is right, I will walk up that driveway and I will knock on that door and take you in my arms and forgive you. I'll marry Radhi, tell her how much of a fool I was and still am but that I love her, more than anything and I wouldn't choose anyone else to spend my life with. I'll mend all your broken hearts. I promise.

I used to think everything was temporary in this world. But then someone told me the truth, the real truth that everyone looks for behind their feigned joy and their overwhelming lives. Some things last. They really do. I hope this does as well.

See you soon
Fahad